Edward Dannreuther

Richard Wagner

his tendencies and theories

Edward Dannreuther

Richard Wagner
his tendencies and theories

ISBN/EAN: 9783337385767

Printed in Europe, USA, Canada, Australia, Japan

Cover: Foto ©Andreas Hilbeck / pixelio.de

More available books at **www.hansebooks.com**

Richard Wagner:

His Tendencies and Theories.

BY

EDWARD DANNREUTHER.

"L'art attend avec impatience une impulsion organique, susceptible à la fois de régénérer sa propre vitalité, et de déployer ses eminents attributs sociaux."--A. Comte, 6, 273.

LONDON :

AUGENER & CO., 86, NEWGATE STREET,

1873.

[Dans un cas quelconque, soit privé, soit public, l'état d'examen ne saurait être évidemment que provisoire, comme indiquant la situation d'esprit qui précède et prépare une décision finale, vers laquelle tend sans cesse notre intelligence, lors même qu'elle renonce à d'anciens principes pour s'en former de nouveaux.—*A. Comte*, "*Philosophie Positive*," 46ème leçon.]

EVER since the first performance of *Tannhäuser* at Dresden in 1845, the poet and composer, Richard Wagner, has been the "best-abused" man in Europe. Competent and incompetent critics, fighting under every manner of flag, have assaulted the "musician of the future" or broken a lance in his honour. The *Almanach des Deutschen Musikvereins* for 1869 gives a surprisingly extensive list of books, pamphlets, and articles, put forth by Germans on the defensive side alone. As far as Germany is concerned, where every one can procure and read the master's own expositions of his views, it would seem absurd that so much ink and paper should be wasted ; but in England, where a genuine curiosity has only of late arisen, concerning the æsthetic problems mooted by Wagner and his disciples, it may be well to make an attempt at elucidating them.

There are three facts, I believe, to which nearly all the pen-and-ink quarrels concerning Wagner can be traced. First, that he published his criticisms and abstract theories at a time when his *later* works of art, by which alone these theories could receive their sanction, were little known, and but rarely and inadequately performed; secondly, that the social and political heresies, which he propounded by way of clearing the air and finding free-breathing space for his artistic ideals, frightened people; and, lastly, that he now and then thought fit to point his moral by attacking living men of repute—Meyerbeer, for instance—in a most savage and merciless manner.

Any one who has watched the spiritual career of an artist of genius, living or dead, will have observed that his theoretical convictions concerning his art throughout his life are a sort of running comment upon his artistic productions. There can be no greater mistake than to suppose that Wagner has written his musical dramas in accordance with any preconceived artistic theories more or less eccentric. He has, like all men of strong creative impulse, trodden the long, dim path from more or less instinctive production to a complete mastery of means and ends. His theories and his practice grew together, and, if anything, the former are a result of the latter. Wagner is a poet first and foremost, and his case differs from that of his predecessors only inasmuch as he gave to the world a more elaborate and minute account of the mental fermentation which preceded and accompanied his works ; and that he has done this ought to entitle him to the thanks of all men who know a poet to be something different from a mere funnel through which the gods pour beautiful thought. He possesses, in common with Goethe, the very rare gift of becoming perfectly conscious of all his mental evolutions, and of being able to give a cool and complete account, an outsider's view as it were, even of his passions. This makes him so formidable as a poet and writer. He speaks always at first hand, talks of nothing but what he has himself seen or felt, and holds his subjects with an intense and passionate grasp. Here is no filtration of other men's ideas, no pouring of other men's thoughts from phial to phial. It was the conflict between his strong artistic desires and the only existing means of realising them which for a time tormented and paralyzed him, and then perforce drove him to criticism. He felt his way through a maze of theoretical speculation on the musical stage, and its elements, mimetics, music and poetry, out of which he came forth, after a protracted and laborious search, with his sight strengthened in more ways than one, and his artistic powers increased a hundredfold.

About the importance of accurate critical insight to a modern artist there can scarcely be two opinions. I quote Charles Baudelaire, "Tous les grands poètes deviennent naturellement fatalement critiques. Je plains les poètes que guide le seul instinct; je les crois incomplets; il serait prodigieux qu'un critique devint poète, et il est impossible qu'un poète ne contienne pas un critique." Mr. Matthew Arnold, too, often preaches on the same text. In his luminous essay on *The Functions of Criticism at the Present Time* he points out the immense mark made by Goethe, not only upon German but upon European thought, contrasts it with the comparatively traceless apparition of Byron on the English horizon, and shows that Goethe has such weight as a poet, not because his productive power was greater, but because his critical exertions and those of his contemporaries gave him a stronger and surer foothold. Among living men one could not find a better illustration of this than Wagner. His principal theoretical books were published between 1849 and 1852, when he was banished from Germany, and had no hope whatever of seeing one of his new dramas embodied on the stage. They raised a paper war, in comparison to which the Parisian squabble in the last century between the *Gluckists* and *Piccinists* appears as one of frogs and mice. Ingenious critics, killing two birds with one stone, contrasted his theories with his *earlier* operas, pointed out plentiful contradictions, and proved both to be the outcome of a confused and extravagant head. Some asserted that he was a mere *charlatan*, who invented theories as a cloak to cover his musical impotence; others that he was a musical genius led astray by metaphysical will o' wisps; a third set, by far the noisiest, held him up to public loathing as a furious madman, who would tear down all existing art fabrics, and plant himself on the ruins "a god of the future." In one respect, and in one only they were unanimous; that a strait-waistcoat would benefit him greatly.

Since 1870, when *Der fliegende Holländer* was produced at Drury Lane, there have been with us many indications of a reaction in Wagner's favour. Nevertheless, it would seem that as yet we have not quite got rid of the old stereotype cries—here charlatan, there genius— which have so long embittered party strife. Of the two appellatives, neither is much to my taste; yet if one must take a side—and the questions involved are too important for any artist to remain neutral—I unhesitatingly choose the latter.

I would limit the designation "genius" to that artistic power which withdraws from the tutorship of existing institutions and reigning dogmas; refuses to support crumbling and falling artistic forms; strikes out new paths for itself, and breathes new life into them. As Walt Whitman has it (Preface to "Leaves of Grass"), "The clearest expression is that which finds no sphere worthy of itself, and makes one."

It appears excessively superficial to judge that we have fathomed any special artistic power if we call it genius, and it is absurd to suppose that Nature throws the precious gift about *a piacere*, so that it often reaches the wrong man. That which distinguishes an artistic temperament is in the first instance little beyond an inborn readiness and aptitude to receive and retain impressions. An *inartistic* person, a *Philistine* of any land or time, can be described as one who meets all impressions from without with an inward reserve, that helps him to see his surroundings only in relation to himself, and never himself in relation to these surroundings ; one who, in Mr. Arnold's phrase, is ready to believe that the donkey was invented so that he might have ass's milk for breakfast, and who, in course of development, attains the sublime height of being able to calculate the exact number of sixpences, and the exact amount of admiration from brother *Philistines*, which his reserve is likely to bring. On the other hand, an artistic character will be found to possess at all events one unmistakable quality : he surrenders himself entirely and without reserve to all impressions which touch him sympathetically. Such impressions will be more or less intense according to the strength of his receptive power, and he will feel compelled to communicate them to others, as soon as he has received more than he can contain. In two directions a surcharge of this sort can flow forth, just as it happens to be the result of impressions from past and contemporary art alone or of impressions from *life* superadded to these. In the first, a direction which

Wagner calls "the feminine," we find most artists of our decenium, poets, painters, and especially sculptors and musicians ; artistic impressions absorb their receptive power so completely, that impressions *from life*, coming later, find its capacity exhausted. These artists live in an art-world entirely separated from life, a world in which art plays with itself, sensitively withdrawing from all contact with actuality, not only from the present state of things, but from all real life in general—in which art looks upon life as an enemy and antagonist, and holds any attempt to embody it to be unbecoming and fruitless. Need I add "modern instances" of to these "wise saws?"

In the other direction, "the male, the creative direction," as Wagner calls it, the power of receiving impressions from life is not by any means weakened, but rather, and in the highest sense too, strengthened by the previously developed artistic power. Life itself is taken up in accordance with artistic impressions, and that power which, from this over-abundance of impressions of both life and art combined, compels its possessor to communicate what he has conceived to others, that power surely is the truly poetic. It does not separate itself from actuality ; it tries rather to embody life from an artistic point of view. Goethe and his works illustrate the latter case perfectly. Of course this is not a question as to whether an artist should treat subjects of the present day or of remote times. True poets will follow the bent of their genius in spite of every absurd pretention on the part of unproductive critics to dictate the choice of subject matter. The contrast I point at lies solely between the *immediate vividness* of a poet's perceptions of the actual facts of life, regardless of whether he chooses to embody them in mythical, legendary, personal, or even political matter; and of his working with a *dim consciousness* of these actualities, such as can be derived from the study of the artistic works of his predecessors. In a word, whether he sees with his own eyes, or blinks through the coloured glasses of other men's minds. On the one hand, the work produced will be of original and strong vitality, on the other, though the technical expression may have reached an equal perfection, its reflected light will burn dimly and go out before long.

To Wagner at his birth the gods gave two gifts—a capacity to receive and to retain the most various and the most intense impressions, and, as he phrases it, "*der nie zufriedene Geist der stets auf neues sinnt*" (the never satisfied spirit that ever seeks new things). Perhaps, by virtue of these two gifts, he also may be labelled "genius."

There is a good deal of empty talk current about the impossibility of one individual's combining the two extremes of poetic creator and dissecting critic, and it has been frequently used as the basis of attacks on Wagner. As though an artist of any brains could in our day help being a critic! No man can escape the bewildering influence of the numberless conflicting theoretical and critical notions and no-notions afloat. There is too much which he is bound to examine and reject ere he can hope to stand on his own legs. He is perforce compelled to clear the air before he can see an inch ahead with whatever eyes the Fates have blessed him, and to do this effectually he wants criticism— critical insight of the keenest sort. Doubtless, a weakling may have his brains trained and criticised out of him; but the highest culture and most elaborate training is apt to chasten and strengthen rather than to mar the originality of a man of genuine powers. Careless and *naïve* production is, in modern times, only pos-

sible when an artist lives in the atmosphere of a
school. As long as he has no desire to soar
above this atmosphere, he knows exactly what
is required of him. He receives his artistic
form ready-made, and he says well-known things
in well-known ways, as well or better than his
predecessors or contemporaries. But in our
day where is there a school of dramatists or
musicians, of painters or poets, that has enough
vitality to satisfy a man of high and intense
aspirations? Wagner, as I have already said,
is a poet first and foremost, who became, and
again ceased to be a critic. In early youth he
produced musical and poetical works for the
concert-room and the stage, some of which were
performed successfully. As he grew riper his
perceptions of possible artistic perfection so
developed themselves, that he felt the operatic
theatre as it existed, and still exists, to be
utterly insufficient. He was then for the first
time in his career compelled to give himself
a distinct account of his position as an artist,
and so, *nolens volens*, he was driven to
criticism.

But this critical tendency is not one peculiar
to Wagner alone, though with no musician has
it borne such fruit. Our whole age feels it.

" In all directions men go back to scrutinise the actual instincts and forces which rule our life, to get behind them, and to see them as they really are, to connect them with other instincts and forces, and thus to enlarge our whole view and rule of life." Philosophy generally, and philosophy of art particularly, is more than ever needed ; and it is, in short, a strong philosophical power, coupled with abnornally pronounced capabilities of receiving and retaining impressions from actual life, that form the indispensable characteristics of every great modern artist.

Most deviations of opinion on art matters, like nearly all conflicting assertions concerning human life and things, depend upon those fundamental philosophic conceptions which men have adopted, either with or without previous examination. Wagner, in his earlier days, before Schopenhauer's profound pessimistic philosophy had illumined his mental horizon and matured his conception of men and things, nourished himself enthusiastically upon Ludwig Feuerbach's optimistic anthropological views ; he was ready, with Feuerbach, to look upon the idea of God as the shadow of the soul of man, to find the kernel of all religions to be man pure

and simple, and to see in art the ultimate outcome and final flower of terrene things. He
looked upon what he calls "*Das Drama,*" in
which man contemplates his own nature in all
its dignity, as the highest and, properly speaking,
the only adequate artistic expression of har-
moniously developed humanity; and the conditions, in many respects new, under which he
conceived it possible to realise "a drama"
that shall expand together with ever-growing
humanity, form the main contents of his theoretical writings. In his pamphlets, "Kunst und
Revolution," and especially in "Das Kunstwerk
der Zukunft," his gyrations round this centre of
drama are of enormous width, and flavour not
a little of social and artistic Utopias; but in
his largest work, "Oper und Drama," in the
"Brief an einem Französischen Freund," and in
"Deutsche Kunst und Politik," the circles contract into more manageable limits, and he aims
at comparatively direct and practical ends. The
trouble with these most interesting books of his,
which for the most part must be looked upon as
running comments upon his efforts at original
artistic creation, is, as with most of the best
German literary productions, that they can
hardly bear condensation; they want elucidation,

illustration, and translation into a more popular phraseology rather than further compression.

In our time art, be it poetry, painting, music, or what not, has little or no connection with, or influence upon, national life. It is with us a sort of hot-house plant, flourishing, it is true, with exuberant vitality here and there, yet belonging exclusively to professional artists, and to those few cultivated amateurs whose faculties have been specially trained to appreciate it. The case seems to have been very different in ancient Greece, where the inner and outer life of the whole nation was shadowed forth in the great union of all the arts upon the tragic stage, and where again the exquisite sense for beauty and proportion, for high and noble thought and action, and for perfect expression of these, seems to have reacted upon both the form and the spirit of national and individual existence. Wagner connects the rapid decay of the Greek drama, which occurred directly after its wondrous successes in the hands of Æschylus, Sophocles, and others, and the subsequent scattering of the great dramatic unity of arts into various branches—*i.e.*, rhetoric, sculpture, painting, music, &c.—with the diminution of political and individual liberty, and the gradual decline of the Greek states. He lays great stress upon the fact that the different arts in separate and isolated cultivation, however much their powers of expression may have been increased and developed by men of brilliant genius since the *renaissance*, could never, without degenerating into unnaturalness and downright faultiness, aim in any way at replacing that all-powerful work of art, the production of which had only been possible by their combined efforts. Aided by the works of eminent art-critics—for instance, Lessing's researches concerning the limits of painting and poetry—Wagner arrives at the result that each separate branch of art, having developed itself to the full extent of its capabilities, cannot overstep these limits without incurring the risk of appearing incomprehensible and fantastical; and he points to the aberrations in which we find modern music under the hands of Berlioz, where it tries to accomplish what poetry alone can do, or to the latest French operas *à la Meyerbeer*, where it tries to construct a drama out of its own means, by way of proof. It appears to him evident that each art, as soon as it has reached its utmost limits, imperatively demands to be joined to a sister art, and, what is more, will be ready to forego its pretensions at accomplishing that which lies ostensibly beyond its natural sphere. His sanguine hopes for the artistic future of Europe are based, on the one side, upon a universal social regeneration, and, on the other, upon the extraordinary and altogether unprecedented development *music,* (which as <u>we</u> understand it was entirely unknown to the Greeks,) has made in the last three centuries. It is the wonderful and apparently limitless capacities for emotional expression Beethoven has given to the art, that have opened to Wagner vistas of dramatic possibilities, such as the ancient world can have had no conception of.

His great problem then, or rather the problem of the art-work of the future as he calls it, somewhat like the social problem of Comte, is this : how can the scattered elements of modern existence generally, and of modern art in particular, be united and interfused in such wise that their rays, issuing from all and every side, shall be concentrated into one luminous focus so as to form an adequate expression of the vast whole—with its eager impulse and enhanced aspirations, its violent convulsions and paroxysms of pain, its love, joy, and humanitarian faith ? This is the first instance. And secondly : what hope of a reaction in favour of nobler, richer, and higher forms of social and individual life than our present wretchedly prosaic industrialism would the creation and acceptance of such a work of art hold out?

Wagner, standing upon Beethoven's supreme achievement, is, from the musician's starting-point, trying to do that for the drama which neither Goethe nor Schiller succeeded in, though their ideal tendency certainly culminated in that direction—*i.e.*, to make it independent of all purely intellectual motives and elements, and to construct it so that it shall appeal and speak at once direct to the feelings of all men of poetical perception, without standing in need of an elaborate mental preparation. It need hardly be added that it is only with the aid of music—that is to say, music in its full maturity, and with its almost superhuman powers of emotional expression, as Beethoven represents it—that such a thing can be accomplished; and it is this feat of leading the full stream of Beethoven's music into a *dramatic* channel, so that it shall fulfil and complete the poetical intentions of a dramatist, that constitutes the principal act of Wagner's genius.

The incalculable importance of an artistic

form, such as is here shadowed forth, would of course consist in the fact that, being free from the restraint of narrow nationality, it might become universally intelligible. As regards literature, the attainment of this quality is out of the question by reason of the diversity of European languages; but in music, the language understood by all men, we possess the requisite equalizing power which, resolving the language of intellectual perception into that of feeling, makes a universal communication of the innermost artistic intuitions possible ; more especially if such communication could, by means of the plastic expression of a dramatic performance, be raised to that distinctness which the art of painting has hitherto claimed as its exclusive privilege.

Need I state here, by way of parenthesis, that " the music of the future," understood in the sense of music that is ugly to us, but may possibly sound all right to our grandchildren, is a bugbear invented by an ingenious critic— Herr Bischoff, or some such worthy, of Cologne, I believe—and which does not in any way represent the *punctum saliens* of the wished-for reformation of dramatic art ?

After what has been said of his general

tendencies, it would be superfluous to enlarge upon the fact that Wagner cannot and
does not regard his later works, which are certainly conceived and executed from this point
of view, ("Die Meistersinger von Nürnberg,"
"Tristan und Isolde," and "Der Ring des
Nibelungen;" a trilogy with a preparatory
evening, consisting of "Das Rheingold," "Die
Walküre," "Siegfried," and "Götterdämmerung"), great and sublime though they be, as
more than the precursors, or rather the germs,
of a new era in art. What he has done is
to give an impulse of immense breadth and
power, and it remains to be seen how far his
titanic push will be felt. I, for my part, am
convinced that its magnitude is too great to be
ever ignored, and it is to him, more than to
any other living poet, that I would apply Walt
Whitman's prophetic words, "Here the theme
is creative, and has vista. Here comes one
among the well-beloved stone-cutters, and plans
with decision and science, and sees the solid
and beautiful forms where there are now no
solid forms."

" Weh ! weh !
Du hast sie zerstört,
Die schöne Welt,
Mit mächtiger Faust ;
Sie stürzt, sie zerfällt !
Ein Halbgott hat sie zerschlagen !
Wir tragen
Die Trümmer ins Nichts hinüber,
Und klagen
Ueber die verlorne Schöne.
Mächtiger
Der Erdensöhne,
Prächtiger
Baue sie wieder,
In deinem Busen baue sie auf !
Neuen Lebenslauf
Beginne,
Mit hellem Sinne,
Und neue Lieder
Tönen darauf !"   *Goethe, " Faust."*

IF I had an unsophisticated friend to whom I wished to prove with an *argumentum ad rem* the faultiness, nay, utter absurdity, of the dramatic grimace known as *grand opera*, I would take him to a performance of Meyerbeer's *Robert le Diable*, believing as I do that it is easiest to point a moral from extreme cases, and that fundamental mistakes in the construction of this particular form of art will be most glaringly apparent, and consequently best recognised, in a representative work such as *Robert*, wherein all the possibilities of artistic, or rather operatic, good and evil, which may have been latent in the form, are developed to their uttermost limits. Far be it from me to underrate the many divinely beautiful things we owe to those musicians of genius, whose names are inscribed on the copious and glorious roll of operatic composers. I am inclined to value the influence which has been exercised by the dramatic stage upon modern music, and even upon the development of pure instrumental music, where there is apparently no chance for any such influence, more highly than has hitherto been done. But it is just the phenomenon, so astonishing and difficult to account for, of the supremely beautiful bits an opera now and then offers, coupled with the sterile and stupid trivialities of the remaining nine-tenths of it, that has opened Wagner's eyes, on the one hand, to the incommensurable possibilities of artistic perfection to be attained by a just combination of the dramatic art with our best modern Beethovenian music, and on the other to the downright detestability of the *genre* called opera.

The real question before us is not one concerning the greater or smaller capacity of this or that composer for the invention of lovely and significant melodies to be sung upon the lyric stage, but rather concerning the *form* in which it was thought imperatively necessary to embody these melodies. Musicians of talent, directly after or even before the rise of the secular cantata and opera at the close of the sixteenth century, have written highly expressive music, and they must undoubtedly have had singers at their disposal capable of interpreting it with becoming warmth. In the works of every musician who has left any trace of his existence we meet with beautiful and expressive phrases. But whilst the symphony, the quartett, and the sonata—sprung from seeds of primitive peoples' dance and song—have been so enriched and enlarged as to make one of Beethoven's great instrumental works appear like a flower-crowned plant which has reached its ultimate perfection and stands revealed complete in all its beauty, the narrow and puerile forms of *aria* and of dry *recitative*, the main props of our operatic music, are to this day as weak and as barren as they were at the outset. They have imposed their heavy and paralyzing fetters upon all and every composer who has approached the stage; and, what is worse, they have shackled and maimed every poet who has attempted to furnish a dramatic poem for music—nay, they have literally crushed him. The situations he was allowed to make use of became typical, the characters lifeless, and the sentiments vapid. Even Goethe, who, as well as Lessing and Schiller, was theoretically inclined to expect most favourable results from the opera, felt constrained to place himself on the level of the *genre*, and deemed it advisable to tune his imagination down to the lowest possible pitch, and turn up puerile and weak trash " for music." " *Ce qui est trop sot pour être dit, on le chante,*" sneered Voltaire.

Let us glance at the historical development of the opera, as Wagner sketches it in his " Oper und Drama." We have seen that in ancient Greece the drama was a direct fruit of the poetical instincts and beliefs of the people. The Middle Ages, too, possessed a species of dramatic art ; and it is easy, in the miracle play and its concomitants, to point out traces of a natural union of poetry and mimetics with music. But it is not in the miracle play, or in anything else emanating directly from the people, that we must look for the origin of the opera. It was at the luxurious courts of Italy—curiously enough the only highly cultivated European country wherein the drama has not reached a really significant height—it was in Italy that the higher classes first began to encourage professional singers to sing *airs*—*i.e.*, people's songs *minus* the ineffable, naïve charm of real *Volkslieder*—for which verses and a sort of dramatic scaffolding were *bon gré, mal gré* manufactured, so as to string them together and give them an appearance of connection

The *dramatic cantata*, then, which aimed at all manner of things except genuine drama, is the true mother of our opera; and the further opera was developed from this point, that is to say, the more rapidly the *aria* became exclusively a basis for the display of vocal agility, the more distinctly it came to be the poet's business, whose assistance was retained for this musical *divertissement*, to content himself with concocting the necessary number of verses to be composed and sung. It is the principal claim to consideration of Metastasio in the last century, of Scribe, the late Mr. Chorley, or any other purveyor of "words for music" in this, that they were the humble servants of all musical conventionalities, and that they tortured and twisted whatever little poetical originality they may have possessed on that Procrustean bed of *aria, scena,* and *finale* whereon we have all been so often stretched and tormented.

For the sake of change in the amusements, a *ballet* was added to the dramatic cantata. Here again, the dance tune was as much an imitation of the people's dance as the *aria* was of the people's tune; and here again it was an obsequious poet's business to combine these two and exhibit them from his dramatic scaffolding; which, as there was not a shadow of necessity for the combination, must have been an awkward task, to say the least of it. The only chance open to him for effecting the desired union was to make use of the musically recited dialogue.

But the *recitative* also, far from being a novel invention resulting from a genuine effort in the direction of the drama made by opera, had been used for centuries in the church for the more effective rendering of Biblical and ritualistic texts; and, as a matter of course, the ritualistic succession of notes soon became on the stage as much stereotyped and as *banale* as they had been in the church.

Thus the three factors of opera, *recitative, aria,* and *ballet,* were determined and fixed upon once for all, and have undergone no organic transformation, though one of them, the *aria*, has been turned to account in various ways, and has suffered, as far as its outward appearance and ornaments are concerned, as many changes of fashion as any tailor's lay figure. And, inevitably, the dramatic scaffoldings supplied by an operatic poet were petrified, and remained dry and sterile. Taken, as they were for the most part, from the world of Greek myths and heroes, as this world was reflected under the wigs of pompous yet sentimental *roccoco* worthies, they were not in the slightest degree calculated to awaken warmth and sympathy in the heart of any listener; but they had the dubious advantage of being fit to be used, like apothecaries' recipes, by an unlimited number of musicians who happened to have mastered the technicalities of their art; and thus it came to pass that scores of favourite *libretti* were set to music over and over again by different persons.

We have heard much of the dramatic revolution so triumphantly accomplished by Gluck. I have never been able to see that it consisted in anything beyond what Wagner describes it to be, a revolt against the supremacy of dramatic singers, and an attempt to place music in direct *rapport* with the sentiment expressed by the words, with the character of the persons singing, and even with the particular accents and peculiar inflexions of the language used. Gluck turned his singers consciously and on principle into mere spokesmen of his dramatic and musical intentions; and his imperishable and distinctive merit lies in the fact that he grasped these intentions passionately, and gave to them, by the side of the direct artistic expression, as a record of which his French operas are immortal, also an abstract and theoretical enunciation. But as regards *form*—and this, as has already been insisted upon, is in such cases the vital point, much more than the greater or lesser degree of warmth and artistic fire with which a composer has accomplished his task—on this vital point of form he has left things just as he found them. Airs, recitatives, and dance tunes each enjoy their separate and isolated existence in his works, just as they did with his grandfathers. His operas are like theirs, conglomerates of more or less finished pieces of music, rather than organisms of which a distinct dramatic action is the kernel and music the last and the most powerful means of expression. Gluck's poets were more than ever his *très-humbles serviteurs.* They translated the master-works of the Louis XIV. tragedy into the current opera jargon.

All that can by any possibility be accomplished in the musical drama from the musician's specific point of view, and without taking the poet into consideration, was accomplished by Gluck's successors, Cherubini, Méhul, and Spontini. They have widened, without destroying, the musical forms to the utmost ; they maintained the traditional arrangement of the *aria;* they rendered the recitative and the connecting links between it and the aria more expressive ; and, what is of especial importance, they allotted the execution of the airs to more than one person, according to dramatic necessities, so that the character of monologue hitherto essential to all operas was got rid of. Of course duetti and terzetti had been in use long before their time ; but the fact that they rendered these, which had formerly been mere slight modifications of the solo aria, subservient to the higher purpose of *dramatic musical ensemble,* this was the progress which these great men realised ; and it would be difficult, remarks Wagner, "to answer them, if they now perchance came amongst us, and asked in what respect we had improved on their mode of musical procedure."

Cherubini and his friends had allowed the poet to develop his art in the exact ratio of their own increase of musical freedom and strength; but with them also he never rose above the position of a subordinate.

It may seem strange that nothing has yet been said of Mozart, the most gifted and the most musical of all musicians—he whose unlimited powers and inexhaustible fecundity left an indelible mark on the history of his art, and whose greatest efforts towards its development are to be found precisely in his operas. I have chosen this place to introduce Mozart's name, as it is with his glorious works for the stage that Wagner believes he can best illustrate the present thesis. Mozart was further removed from the chance or the temptation to make innovations resulting from 'critical reflections on his art than any other great musician before or since. Yet it is in the opera, where in point of form he gives us so little that is new, that we meet with his most absolutely original creations—creations which are by far grander than his best pieces of instrumental music—creations in which he unfolds all the powers of the divine art. And this is exactly the point that lays bare the very kernel of the matter under consideration.

Mozart, the supreme musician, produces his best music there where the poet has given him a worthy chance, and has risen a little above the ordinary *libretto* groove. Mozart possessed more than any other musician the subtlest and deepest instinctive knowledge of the nature of his art; he knew for certain that it was an art of expression only, of the sublimest and most perfect expression, still of expression, and nothing beyond. To his honour be it said, it was impossible for him to make poetical music if the poetical groundwork was null. He could not write music to *Titus* equal to *Don Juan*, to *Cosi fan tutte* equal to *Figaro*. Good music he always wrote, but beautiful music only when he was inspired. His inspiration certainly came from within, but it never shone so bright as when it was lighted from without. Wagner expresses his conviction more than once that Mozart would, with his supreme instinct, have solved the problem of a real musical drama; but, as it was, he could only give the truest and the most intense expression to the airs, duets, and ensemble pieces which his fabricators of libretti handed to him. He has attested the inexhaustible puissance of music as a means of expression better than Gluck and any of his successors; but, in the main, he also leaves the traditional operatic forms as he found them.

Weber, the noble, high-spirited, and chevalresque, seems to have made for himself, in the long course of his services as conductor of the Opera at Prague and Dresden, a practical analysis of operatic melody. He perceived almost instinctively that it was in the first instance based upon the people's song, and in his endeavours to revivify it, he was tempted to take up the *Volsklied* of Germany and to transplant it bodily into his operas. The predominance of long-drawn, joyous, yet tender and melodious phrases, as distinguished from the short, bold, and eccentric rhythms peculiar to nationalities like the Polish and Hungarian, is the special characteristic of the German *Volsklied*. One cannot fancy German songs without accompaniment. They are usually sung in at least two parts, and one is involuntarily tempted to complete the harmony by adding the bass and the remaining middle part. Whatever chance of excellence a dramatic poem offered that could by any possibility be resolved into and expressed by this melody was safe in Weber's hands ; but we have only to glance at *Euryanthe*, his most ambitious and in some respects his most beautiful work, to see how he tortured himself, and tried in vain to express what could not and would not amalgamate with this melody ; and where Weber's genius failed who shall hope to succeed ?

So far we have dealt with the serious aspect of the matter ; let us now look at the frivolous side.

With Rossini, and in an increased ratio with his successors, the history of the opera is simply that of operatic melody; as Wagner has it— "naked, absolute, ear-tickling melody, which one sings and whistles, without knowing wherefore ; which one exchanges to-day for that of yesterday, and forgets again to-morrow, for no reason whatsoever ; which sounds melancholy when we are amused, and joyous when we are disgusted ; and which we hum apropos of any and everything." Take Rossini's works all in all, and you have numberless operatic melodies of here and there an immensely effective sort, but comparatively very little beyond. His object has evidently been to pour forth multitudes of pleasing tunes, such as are fit to be whistled and sung by all the world. If he occasionally gives a powerful dramatic effect, one hails it as something unexpected ; for, as a rule, an opera of his is like a string of beads, each bead being a glittering and intoxicating tune. Dramatic and poetic truth, and all that makes a stage performance interesting, is sacrificed to tunes. The task of the composer of Italian opera, after Rossini, came to be little beyond that of manufacturing variations on one fixed type of *aria* for this or that particular singer. And, together with the advent of Rossini, the operatic public in general—that most equivocal of all publics : " *Combien faut-il de sots pour faire un public ?* "*—became the sole arbiter of artistic reputation, the ultimate court of appeal in questions of artistic excellence, its taste the sole guide for artistic production, and its favourite purveyor of tunes the autocrat of the whole operatic entertainment.

Properly speaking, then, the opera ends with Rossini. It was virtually at an end as soon as the principle that melody without character, and of the shallowest and most *banale* type, was the very essence of music, and that the loosest connection of one operatic tune

* Chamfort.   D

with another was musical form, had been practically set up and accepted. Auber, and Meyerbeer in his Parisian productions after him, made melodic experiments. Auber listened intently to the *couplets* and *contredanses* (*i.e.*, the can-can) danced and sung by his compatriots, imported besides melodies from Italy and elsewhere, and served them up intact. The enormous success of his *Muette de Portici*, a work which marks an epoch on the French stage, and wherein he unquestionably takes a flight far higher, as regards intensity of effect and originality of musical treatment, than in his numerous productions for the *Opéra Comique*, tempted Rossini to take a leaf out of the same book. Thenceforth *Guillaume Tell* and *Massaniello* were the centres round which the operatic world gyrated until the coming of the great *Robert le Diable*, who "danced awa'" with them both. Meyerbeer screamed at the top of his voice what Rossini and Auber had been saying, and, turning his artistic attainments and experience, both enormous, to account on purely commercial principles, he managed to outdo them both. Instead of sympathy with the inflexions of any particular tongue, which he did not possess, he had acquired the knack of

" setting " every European language—that is to say, of drowning its cadences in the shallow and noisy stream of his music. He studied with the attention that a stock-jobber gives to a new prospectus the scores of Hector Berlioz, that astonishing virtuoso of the orchestra and of orchestration, that greatest of French romanticists, with whom the last mystical works of Beethoven had brought forth such strange fruit : and taking Rossini's melodies as a *point d'appui*, he managed to concoct the most unpalatable musical phenomenon of our day—a glittering kaleidoscope of eccentric sounds and effects—his *grand opéra*. On his banner was inscribed *la caractéristique—i.e.*, " the dodge " of disguising frivolous and empty tunes in a garb that shall appear significant. My unsophisticated friend above mentioned, if he did chance to witness a performance of *Robert le Diable*, would be scared by the queer agglomerate of effects—the most ethereal and the most drastic —the most far-fetched and the most commonplace—refinement and vulgarity, sensuality and religion—a veritable *olla podrida*—" *Wer vieles bringt wird manchem etwas bringen und jeder geht zufrieden aus dem Haus*," as the director puts it in *Faust*. In an eloquent peroration towards the end of the first part of his " Oper und Drama," Wagner, after having spoken of Meyerbeer's specific musical gifts and set them down as comparatively insignificant, speaks in most enthusiastic terms of certain bits of supremely beautiful dramatic effect in Meyerbeer's works—fragments, for instance, of the great love-duet in *Les Huguenots*, and particularly of the wonderfully expressive melody in G flat major towards the close of it. This and similar bits, let us not forget, occur only there where the poet has supplied genuine poetical motives, and thus tend to prop our thesis.

But besides being "characteristic," operatic melody became "historical." Have we not got our chorus dressed in all manner of historical costumes, with decorations to match ? Does not the theatrical tailor produce both cut and colour with scrupulous exactitude ? What matter if the music be dull, spite of its pretentious peculiarities, as long as its uncouth *tournure* passes for historical ? We have consumed the tunes and costumes of all civilised countries, Oriental and Occidental, for the sake of being " characteristically national and historical." Why should we not have red ochre and scalps, and the war-whoop with an accompaniment of tomahawks and rattling wampum, in course of the next operatic decennium ?

To resume. Gluck, as we have seen, consciously tried to speak correctly and intelligibly in music; he never disfigured a verse for the sake of musical development, and he rendered whatever emotional elements he found in his texts as completely as possible. Mozart spoke "with the perfect rectitude and *insouciance* of the movements of animals, and the unimpeachableness of the sentiment of trees in the woods and grass by the roadside."* Give him dull stuff, and he reproduces dull stuff; give him genuine dramatic feeling, and he returns it to you ennobled and intensified a thousandfold. His music glorifies even the paltriest theatrical conventionalities. The closer you look into the glowing colours of Mozart's operas, the more clearly you will distinguish underneath them the outlines furnished by the poet. Without these outlines, the best part of them is inconceivable. Unhappily, this occasional union of musician and poet disappeared entirely in the course of operatic development. Rossini's cry was "Melody, melody;" and Weber's opposition to him was directed more against the shallowness and frivolity of this melody than against the

* Walt Whitman.

unnatural position which in Italian opera the poet occupied towards the musician. In fact the fire and the fascinating charm of Weber's melody made a still greater autocrat of the musician, and Weber thought himself justified in dictating to Helmine von Chezy, who wrote the libretto of *Euryanthe* for him, not only details of expression, but even the dramatic movements of the characters and the motives for their actions; and in the failure of his favourite *Euryanthe*, which Weber lived to see, we can convince ourselves, better than with any other of his works, that his twofold aim, " abso-lute melody "—melody which shall be sufficient in itself—and dramatic expression which shall be true and just throughout, are irreconcilable.

When we talk of the opera now, we talk not of a work of art, but of a thing *à la mode*— a fashion. For my own part, the popular opera of our day strikes me as the last ghastly grin of a galvanized corpse.

I conclude, therefore, with Wagner, that one or the other, absolute melody or the drama, must be sacrificed. Rossini threw the drama overboard ; and Weber tried to construct it by means of his melody, and failed. Music, which is of all existing means of expressing emotion the most powerful, ought not and cannot on its own account attempt "characteristic, dramatic, or historical" harlequinades.

And we are constrained to admit the incapacity of music unaided by other arts to construct the drama out of its own means, and to assert for the future that music must forego part of its pretensions, and in case of dramatic necessity merge its individuality in the great end of all the arts combined—the drama.

3

" Omnes artes, quæ ad humanitatem pertinent, habent quoddam commune vinculum et quasi cognatione quadam inter se continuantur."

Cicero, " *Pro Archia Poeta*," Cap. I.

WITH all single and separate arts that address themselves solely or in part to our imagination, purity of each is a primary requisite. If too many and heterogenous means are employed, the imagination will deviate from the central point, and the impression intended to be made on us will be blurred and chaotic. But a dramatist in Wagner's sense does not appeal at all to the imagination, but to the *immediate sensuous perception*, and here an intimate union of various arts, poetry, music, mimetics, painting, &c., is supremely intelligible, for it speaks to all our perceptive faculties united. It should, of course, be borne in mind that we are always talking of the drama actually acted, as of a symphony actually played ; both are alive only during the time of actual production, and should be judged as they then present themselves.

We have seen that such operatic composers as "fly at high game" did not and could not realize their aspirations. It has been shown that the cause of their failure is to be sought for in the intrinsic weakness and unnaturalness of the *genre* called opera; and we have been led to assume with Wagner that the *ideal* so ardently striven after, a genuine musical drama, cannot be attained otherwise than by a radical change in the relative position of its two principal components, poetry and music. We have seen that music, when it aspires to the drama, must ally itself closely with poetry; and that, as the supreme art of expression, it must in such case carefully avoid overstepping the boundaries of the task it is so exclusively fitted for, that of evolving flower and fruit from out of the seeds furnished by poetry. It is the object of the present division to point out that, from its side also, dramatic poetry may hope to find its salvation in a close union with music, and moreover to show that it is the unmistakeable tendency of the entire development of European drama since the *renaissance* to effect such a consummation.

In both the form and the subject-matter of all post-*renaissance* plays, we can trace the influence of two entirely distinct and different factors; first and foremost the mediæval romance, with its descendants, the romantic legend and the modern novel; secondly, and as it were *per accidens*, the Greek drama, or rather the formal essence thereof, as abstracted by Aristotle in his " Poetics." We may take as types, on the one hand, Shakespeare, whose plays are for the most part dramatized stories and romances ; and on the other, Racine, who in some sense approaches the Greek drama.

Nothing strikes one more in mediæval poems and romances than the chaotic super-abundance of subject-matter. Whilst reading them one finds it hopeless to trace the changes of time and place, or to keep account of the intricate maze resulting from the restless activity exhibited by the *dramatis personæ*. Yet we have one and all felt the indiscribable charm resulting from such a display of exuberant fancy, and the secret of this charm lies in the fact that a mediæval poet could afford to let his fancy run riot, as he appeals solely and exclusively to the *imagination* of his readers or hearers.

Yet the desire for curtailment, or rather for concentration of this endless material, was sure to be felt sooner or later, and hence we have the phenomenon of the romance being condensed into a play. But however more compact the subject-matter presented by the Elizabethan dramatist might be than the original romances or chronicles from which it is taken, there still remained one fact in connection with the Shake-spearean drama, which left the doors wide open for the introduction of an immense amount of acting matter—such as we meet with in Shakespeare's historical plays, for instance—and this was the fact that in everything that concerns *decoration* it appealed to the *imagination* only. A board, with an inscription that could be easily changed, and a curtain, occupied the place of our elaborate *coulisses*.

When in the last century it was thought advisable to re-attempt the acting of Shakespeare's plays, the public had become so inured to accurate and detailed decorations, that it appeared necessary to the most intelligent actors, Garrick for instance, to change Shakespeare's works so as to suit "modern requirements." Scenes which did not appear absolutely indispensable to the clear understanding of the plot were entirely omitted ; others, again, were condensed or joined together. Against such practices the strongest protests have since been launched by poets and *literati*—protests which are of course unanswerable from a literary point of view, but have no weight whatever with the actors, who point to their stage experience and stand firm. Only two ways seem open to escape the dilemma. Ludwig Tieck, the German poet, proposed the most obvious one—to restore Shakespeare's stage with board and curtain bodily—and this was actually done at Berlin, but proved, like all radical restorations of bygone customs, an utter failure; the other was what has been in the main adopted on the present English and German stages; the whole inexhaustible machinery and the whole luxurious paraphernalia which form an integral part of a *grand opéra*, were brought into play to realize the sudden and frequent changes of scene. Here, then, we are treated to as much reality as is attainable on the stage, but it is a reality far less real than that which holds us captive when we *read* Shakespeare; *then* our imagination performs what is required of it to perfection and with ease; whilst the whole mass of operatic decoration only tends to stun and bewilder us, much as the mediæval romances stun and bewilder their readers with superabundance of matter.

The Italians of the *renaissance* never dreamt of trying to make use of the people's plays for artistic purposes. They took their stand on Aristotle, and, as their performances were contrived for the *salons* of princes, it was found convenient to observe his rules concerning the unity of place and time. The enthusiasm for the writers of antiquity in the highly-cultivated circles of Italian *illuminati* was far too engrossing to let any one dream of dramatizing those popular romances, to escape from the spirit of which was the principal tendency of the whole artistic movement known as the *renaissance*. Even if it had appeared desirable to make some use of them, how could their matter have been condensed to admit of Aristotle's unities? It was thought far wiser to import the ready-made condensations of myths and stories as they are preserved in Greek literature.

So the Italians of the *renaissance*, and the Frenchmen of Louis XIV. after them, remained imitators of antiquity, in so far as they understood it, and their dramatic productions retained the stamp of artificiality. Racine's tragedies are the exact antipodes of Shakespearian plays. Racine's art is rhetorical rather than dramatic; it supplies motives for action without the action proper; it offers the speech upon the stage and the action behind; it gives the will without the deed. The instinct of musicians soon prompted them to turn this prominent rhetorical side of it into musical phraseology, to translate Racine's *tirades* into the *aria;* and it is not too much to say that the French tragedy of Louis XIV. reached its ultimate goal in *Gluck's opera :* the premature musical blossom of an unnatural dramatic plant, reared in an artificial hotbed.

Shakespeare, if he had witnessed the chaotic changes of scenery and decoration with which his plays are now performed, would undoubtedly have been induced to try further condensation of the acting matter, just as time and action of the mediæval people's play had been condensed by himself and his predecessors, and he would probably have discovered, what Schiller and Goethe found in the course of their dramatic experiments—that legendary and historical romance is, after all, unmanageable for the highest dramatic purposes. It is an interesting question whether Shakespeare would have done what the Greeks did—dramatize myths. Wagner answers it in the affirmative, and shows that the *mythos*, in which the poetic perceptions of a whole race are so concentrated as to receive their most palpable and intelligible expression, is the true material for the ideal drama we have in view. It will be necessary to return to this point by-and-by.

Every poet who watched the progress of the drama, with intent to test his powers in it, was compelled to take his choice of two alternatives : either to give up all direct communion with the stage, and to write dramatic poems for the book market and the library, as Goethe did in *Faust*, and as after him Byron, Browning, and Swinburne, in all their dramatic pieces— or to try to make the best of that artificial and, to a modern mind, instinctively uncongenial form, which, as we have seen, was constructed by Italian and French poets, in accordance with Aristotle. We can best trace both sides and influences in the experiments made by the two greatest of German dramatists, Goethe and Schiller.

Goethe's constructive powers waxed stronger as long as he continued directing it towards the drama, and it decreased and became flabby, when, with failing courage, he withdrew his attention from the stage. He commenced his career as a playwright with dramatizing a full-blooded German romance, " *Götz von Berlichingen*," Shakespeare being avowedly his guide in the treatment of it. He executed it in the first instance much more from the poet's, or rather the poetic student's point of view, than from a dramatist's; and afterwards, when it came to be acted, he was obliged to remodel it so as to suit the exigencies of a practical performance on a stage possessing all the scenical apparatus necessary for a clear presentation of the whereabouts of a dramatic action, over and above the wherewithal—in other words, so as to make it appeal more to the immediate sensuous perceptions of the audience than to the imagination. But under the process of rewriting, the poem lost the freshness of a romance, and did not gain the full strength of a drama; which fact recalls the point made above, that the romance *per se* is unmanageable as the subject matter of a drama. After his experiences with "*Götz von Berlichingen*," Goethe tried *Das bürgerliche Drama* —the home-spun drama—in various small plays, which treated the realities of German middle-class life, much as the novels of the period embodied them; and from this narrow sphere he jumped at once, and with an enormous, a Titanic effort, to *Faust*,—that altogether incommensurable poem—in which he threw over all

connection with the actual stage, and retained
only the advantages of a dramatic exposition.
Goethe after this gave himself no more trouble
about what is called a good acting play; he was
content with the statuesque calm of *Iphigenie*,
and the perfect proportion of artistic work-
manship in *Tasso*. In his *Iphigenie in Tauris*
we have a work as finished *in toto* and in detail
as a piece of Greek sculpture. But he was
able to accomplish this only with materials
ready-made and condensed to his hands, like
the Greek story. Wagner points out, with rare
ingenuity, that, like Beethoven in his symphonies, Goethe dissects the poetic material as
Beethoven dissects the melodious kernel of his
works and reconstructs it organically and anew;
yet Goethe was unable to mould the elements
of modern life into a similarly complete form,
and we find him at various intervals of his
poetic career renouncing the drama and writing
romances to fulfil his ardent desire of embody-
ing the present in some palpable shape. So
it would seem that the poet was unable to
embody the ultimate blossom of his modern
conception of the world in an actual dramatic
performance; he was content to embody it by
means of *descriptions* appealing to the imagina-

E

tion. In his youth he pushed forward with a true Shakespearean impulse towards the drama; yet his most influential artistic creation—*Wilhelm Meister, die Wahlverwandschaften,* the second part of *Faust*—was destined to lose itself into the romance, from which he had started, and into the dramatic poem, not fit and not intended for, actual performance.

Schiller began, as Goethe did, with a dramatized novel (*Die Räuber*) under the influence of Shakespeare; "home-spun" and political romances (*Cabale und Liebe, Fiesko, Don Carlos*) occupied him until he arrived at the very root of these—*history* pure and simple—and he exerted himself to produce a drama (*Wallenstein*) direct from this source, He attempted to condense and colour the historical facts for his stage purposes, but he was not and could not be satisfied with the result. History ceased to be history, yet the ideal drama he aspired to was not realized. He was able to give but a rather unclear extract of history in the main parts of his drama (*Die Piccolomini* and *Wallensteins Tod*), and he had to make a separate picture of the world surrounding his heroes (*Wallensteins Lager*). In this, his most elaborate work, he perceived, and we perceive with

him, that upon the modern stage, which appeals
to the sensuous perceptions more than to the
imagination, historical matter is unmalleable.
Shakespeare, appealing to the spectators' imagination, might and would have given a picture
of the entire Thirty Years' War in the space
occupied by Schiller's trilogy. After *Wallenstein*, Schiller gave his attention more and more
to the antique forms ; and in *Die Braut von
Messina* he actually went to the length of intro-
ducing the Greek chorus and the Greek fate.
When the unsatisfactory result of his experiments led him to despair of finding salvation
in a union of pure Greek form and mediæval
story (a union symbolized by Goethe in his
marriage of *Helena* and *Faust*), he sought in
his last dramatic poem, *Wilhelm Tell*, to save
at least his freshness and vitality as a poet,
which had suffered considerably whilst he was
struggling in the meshes of sterile æsthetical
speculation.

Ever since Schiller, the drama has oscillated
aimlessly and helplessly between the two poles
of antique form and the modern novel. The
dramatic works of our noblest poets—take
Browning as an instance—are certainly not fit
to be acted ; and our acting plays, though we

may accredit them with all manner of virtues, are as certainly not poetical.

To all poetic students, who as a rule keep aloof from actual theatrical performances, and take cognizance of dramatic *literature* only, it is a surprising fact, and one which they deeply deplore, that *the opera has not only absorbed the interest due to the spoken drama*, but has actually exercised the most deteriorating influence on the character of theatrical performances generally. Even actors of high artistic aspirations desire to be "successful" with their *rôles*, they want to make a certain amount of "effect," and they are ready to join in all cries against the opera on seeing mediocre singers enabled to "bring down the house" by means of the commonest and most frivolous musical phrases. It is scarcely fair to blame actors of the ordinary type if they give way to the temptation of imitating some cheap operatic effects, as far as their art can admit of, if they "split the ears of the groundlings" with ranting or the sing-song known as "false pathos."

Few thinking actors or playwrights, however, have cared to follow Wagner when he goes on to point out that these and the like deplorable truths do not cover the whole aspect of the matter, and that it offers other points of view of far higher importance, which hold out glorious hopes for the future.

We have all felt the astounding effect of certain dramatic musical combinations, in the operas of Mozart for instance; we are impressed by these so deeply and firmly, and with an immediate vividness such as no art but music can approach.

Let the admirers of the spoken drama say what they will, it is undeniable that it has been outstripped in public favour by the opera, *and it is more than probable that the opera is destined to furnish the seed from which a veritable ideal drama will spring up.* The noble music of a great master lends to the performance of operatic singers of small natural gifts an indefinable charm, such as even the greatest actor cannot hope to exercise in the spoken drama. On the other hand, a genuinely gifted dramatic performer can ennoble very poor music to such a degree, that we get an impression stronger than any which the same gifted performer could by any chance produce without the aid of music. The mysterious might of the divine art lifts whatever it touches into a sublime sphere.

If, then, the main object of the poetical

career of Goethe and Schiller can be charac-
terized as an attempt to discover the ideal
subject-matter and an ideal form for the modern
drama; and if, as Schiller, in a very curious
confession, records it, with him the beginning
of all poetical production was *eine musikalische
Gemüthsstimmung* (a musical state of mind),
which only after a time brought forth the
poetical idea—pictures and words—if it is a
fact sufficiently proved, best of all in a recent
pamphlet,* that the drama of Æschylos
took its origin from the union of the
older didactic hymns of the Hellenic priests
with the newer Dionysian dithyrambos—that
is to say, *with poetry conceived and executed in
the orgiastic spirit of musical sound*—we may
by analogy confidently conclude and expect
that from out of the spirit of Beethovenian
music and of the manifold branches of Teutonic
mythos, which Wagner conceives to be the true
subject-matter for the supreme work of art
he has in view, an ideal dramatic form will
emanate which will stand in relation to the
spirit of modern existence as the drama of

---

* "Die Geburt der Tragödie aus dem Geiste der Musik," von
Friedrich Nietzsche, Ordentl. Professor der klassischen Philologie
an der Universität Basel.

Æschylos stood in relation to the national spirit of Greece.

I conclude this part of the subject with a summing-up translated from Wagner's *Brief an einem Französischen Freund.* " Referring to the hopes and wishes so frequently expressed by great poets of attaining in the opera an ideal *genre*, I came to believe that the poet's co-operation, so decisive in itself, would be perfectly spontaneous on his part and desired by him. I endeavoured to obtain a key to this aspiration, and thought to have found it in the desire, so natural to a poet, and which in him directs both conception and form, to employ the instrument of abstract ideas—language —in a manner which would take effect on the feelings. As this tendency is already predominant in the invention of poetical subject-matter, and as only that picture of human life may be called poetical in which all motives, comprehensible to abstract reason, only disappear so as to present themselves rather as motives of purely human feeling—in like manner this tendency is obviously the only one to determine the form and expression of poetical execution. In his language the poet tries to substitute the original sensuous signification of words for their abstract and conventional meaning, and by rhythmical arrangement and the almost musical ornament of rhyme in the verse, to assure an effect to his phrases which will charm and captivate our feelings. *This tendency, essential to the poet, conducts him finally to the limits of his art, where it comes into immediate contact with music; and the most complete poetic work would therefore be that which in its ultimate perfection would resolve itself into music."*

4.

Mephistopheles. "Grau, theurer Freund, ist alle Theorie,
Und grün des Lebens goldner Baum."

Goethe, "Faust."

HAVING traced the current of both modern
music and poetry to the point at which it
appeared palpably evident that the one as
well as the other was possessed with a
longing for a complete reunion, having hailed
the opera as a foreshadowing of the future
complete drama, and having shown how Goethe
and Schiller strove for the attainment of an
ideal dramatic form which shall have a purely
human interest and be free from the fetters
of all historic conventionality, appealing to the
feelings of men instead of to their abstract
understanding, and how from their numerous
experiments it results as an inevitable conclu-
sion that with such an end in view, historical
as well as social and political matter, because it
cannot be made to bear the necessary condensation without becoming vague and losing
its character, is unmalleable, we have been
forced to agree with Wagner's assertion, that

the proper material for the construction of such a form is *mythos*, and mythos only.

From this point then Wagner, led by the spirit of music, takes his departure, and proceeds to demonstrate how such mythical matter, the nature of which is always essentially emotional, imperatively demands the great language of emotion, music, for its proper presentation. Having settled once for all that it was the aim of the drama to present, in the most universally intelligible manner, the poet's perception of purely human individualities apart from all conventionality, he goes on to solve the problem of form in detail, and to fix the relation of the various factors of his work to one another.

Here then I ought to be able to draw the curtain, and offer the reader a performance of the master's *Nibelungen* trilogy. That would be the proper way of making the particulars which a ɔ to follow fully intelligible; for it is difficult ɔ consider them other than as comments to that central work of Wagner's life, the emotional effect of which when it is actually performed can be the only just criterion as to their validity. For clearness sake, I shall try to sketch the main points separately.

 General Shape of the Drama.—The mythical

subject-matter has a plastical unity; it is perfectly simple and easily comprehensible, and it
does not stand in need of the numberless small
details, which a modern playwright is obliged
to introduce to make some historical occurrence
intelligible. It is divided into few important
and decisive scenes, in each of which the action
arises spontaneously from out of the emotions
of the actors; which emotions, by reason of the
small number of such scenes, can be presented
in a most complete and exhaustive manner. In
planning these scenes according to the distinctive nature of the mythical subject-matter, *it is
unnecessary to take any preliminary account of
specific musical forms* as the opera has them—
arias, duetts, ensemble pieces, &c.—for as the
myths are in themselves emotional, and as the
dramatist moulds them in accordance with and
and under the influence of the spirit of music,
they resolve themselves, as it were quite spontaneously, into musical diction. No phase of
emotion is touched upon, in any one of the
scenes, which does not stand in some important
relation to the emotion of all the rest; so that
the development of the phases from one another, and their necessary sequence, constitute
the unity of expression in the drama.

Musical Form.—Each of the phases of emotion just spoken of has for its outcome some clearly marked and decided musical expression, some characteristic musical theme; and just as there is an intimate connection betwen the phases of emotion, so an intimate interlacing of the musical themes takes place, which interlacing spreads itself not only over an entire scene or part of a scene, but over the whole extent of the drama. It is never made use of for the display of any purely musical combinations *per se*, but it is always in the closest relationship and most complete union with the poet's dramatic intentions. Thus, that wonderful power by which a great musician can make his phrase undergo metamorphosis after metamorphosis, without losing its character as the expression of some distinct emotion, is here developed to a hitherto unknown extent; and the means of dramatic expression are, in consequence, infinitely widened and enlarged.

Verse.—Concerning this I must beg leave to begin *ab ovo*. Two facts are certain as regards the different means by which poets have tried to enhance the power of everyday language, so as to render it capable of exercising a direct influence on our feelings—

rhythm and rhyme—*i.e.*, regularity and melody; these facts are, firstly, that the poets of the Middle Ages, to attain regularity of rhythm, constructed their verses according to some fixed melody or other; and, secondly, that the condition from which the astonishing and to us incomprehensible variety of Greek metres arose was the inseparable and ever-present combined action of mimetics, or rather, of the movements of an ideal dance, with the poetical language, as it was sung or chanted.

The modern Germans have imitated, as well as their unquestionably flexible language will admit of, every metre under the sun; but no one will deny that the fixed rhythms upon which the German language prides itself so much exist far more for the reader's eye than for the hearer's ear. Take the most common form of verse in modern German—iambics— is it not torture to hear the sense of the language continually forced and twisted to suit this five-footed monster? Sensible actors, when it was first used on the stage, were afraid of its sing-song, and treated it exactly like prose.

Italians and Frenchmen, who have not attempted to base their rhythms upon prosodical longs and shorts, and who have chosen to measure their verse by the number of syllables it contains, have found a rhyme at the end of each verse absolutely necessary. Now, if we examine the relation of music to all the varieties of modern verse, we come across a most curious fact. Musicians declaim German iambics, and indeed every species of verse, in all and every sort of time. As for the rhyme at the end of a line, music, as a rule, swallows it entirely. And the cases wherein the musical rhyme actually corresponds to the rhyme in the verse are for the most part accidental, and, at any rate, few and far between. A musician can do no more with iambics than the actors did ; he must treat them as prose and stretch them to fit his tune.

Seeing that modern versification offers such small attraction, Wagner was led to ask himself what sort of rhythmical speech it might be that was most intimately connected with musical diction, and the answer was not far to seek. Just as we have seen the poetical material condensed by dramatists for their purposes, so the expression of our daily speech will have to be condensed. When we speak under the pressure of some strong emotion, we involuntarily drop conventional phraseology; we contract our accents and enforce them with a raised voice; our words become rhythmical; our expressions terse and to the point. In the early days of all the Teutonic languages, such a manner of speech had been used for artistic purposes; it is the *alliterative* verse of the *Edda*, of *Beovulf*, &c. The condensed form and the close relative position of the accented vowels in alliterative verse give to it an emotional intensity, which renders it peculiarly musical. When a poet conceives this sort of verse—and indeed the fact holds good, though in a lesser degree, with all sorts of verse—he is never without some sense of harmony in connection with the melody of his words. And at this point the musician, whose art enables him to give precise expression to the vaguely conceived harmonies of the poet, steps in; on the basis of this harmony he proceeds to fix the exact melody pertaining to the verse, and thus finally to complete the desire for perfect poetical expression.

Of the three opera-manufacturing nations, the Italians, the French, and the Germans, the latter only possess an everyday speech which has an immediate and easily recognizable connection with its roots. Italians and Frenchmen only come to understand the radical meaning of their speech by studying Latin and other so-called dead languages; it may be said of them that their speech speaks for them, not they through their speech.

Melody.—Wagner's melody has undergone many a metamorphosis. It is only since he was led by the nature of his mythical subjects to adopt the alliterative verse just spoken of, that his manner of procedure has been ultimately determined. In his youth he tried to embody Schumann's maxim, " You must invent original and bold melodies ;" but the more he came to derive his form of musical expression direct from the legendary matter chosen for dramatic presentation, the less he troubled himself to appear " original." In *Rienzi*, his first published opera, we find, with little exception, Italian and French *grand opéra* phraseology *à la Spontini*. In *Der fliegende Holländer*, the story of which is legendary, the melody often approaches the *Volkslied*. It has a rhythmical backbone, as it were, which *Rienzi* lacks. In *Tannhäuser*, and still more in *Lohengrin*, the melody grows from out of the verse. In both these works, it is not so much any melodic

peculiarity as the emotion expressed by the
melodious phrase that attracts the listener.
The fault of modern verse, pointed out above—
its want of real rhythmical precision—inevitably
told upon the melody. But Wagner managed
to increase its power enormously by the em-
ployment of characteristic harmonies. He
individualized it by means of significant accompaniments, and thus rendered it highly
efficient for his dramatic purpose. *Alliterative*
verse has at last given to his melody what
was still wanting — a *rhythmical animation*
which is fully justified by the nature of the
verse. The use of alliteration, and *nota bene*
of the melody springing from it, innovation as
it certainly is, sprang, like all his innovations,
direct from the supreme artistic instinct with
which he masters the subject-matter congenial
to him, and was not in any sense the result
of abstract speculation. Most musicians will
be aware of the fact that if a composer writes
the accompaniments to a vocal phrase in such
a manner that those vocal notes which are
essential to the harmony are omitted in the
instrumental portion, the result is disastrous;
both the vocal and the instrumental parts will
sound incomplete; the fact being that our ear

F

invariably takes special and separate notice of
the human voice, the colour of which is at all
times totally and absolutely distinct and different, from the colour of the orchestral instruments. It is upon this fact that Wagner bases
his procedure ; he allows his vocal melody,
independent of the orchestral melody, to grow
directly from out of the verse. He intends
it to be nothing but an intensified version of
the actual sounds of rhythmical speech. The
relation of this sung melody to the *melos* of

The Orchestra, so difficult to describe, and
so easy to understand if one has the good
fortune to hear it actually executed, Wagner
describes in an elaborate simile, the main points
of which are as follow :—" Let us look upon
the orchestra as a deep mountain lake pierced
to its very depth by the sunlight (*i.e.*, the
poetical intention which moulds endless possibilities of musical harmony to its own particular
purpose), the surrounding banks of which are
visible from every point. From the tree-stems
that grew upon the banks, a skiff was fashioned,
precisely in a manner to render it fit to be
carried on the lake, and to cut through its
waters. This skiff is the melody growing from
out of the verse, sung by the dramatic singer

and supported by the surrounding waves of the
orchestra. It is a skiff totally different from
the lake, yet fashioned solely with a view to
float upon it. Only when it is launched upon
its waves does it become alive ; supported and
carried, yet going of its own will, it attracts
our eyes as we glance across the lake, as though
the sole purpose of the entire show was to offer
this particular picture."

But not only will the orchestra thus carry
the verse ; with its help also the spirit of music
will reveal the innermost emotions of the *dramatis personæ ;* its supremely intelligible speech
will, in unison with expressive mimetics, initiate
us into the secret of those *nuances* and depths
of feeling which all arts except music can only
hint at, and which without its divine aid would
remain absolutely inexpressible. It will speak
to the ear as the actor's movements and the
expression of his features speak to the eye ;
over and above this, it will at the very beginning of the performance put the hearer into the
proper frame of mind to expect the dramatic
pictures and actions to come, and it will recall
all those sounds and phrases belonging to past
scenes which can to some extent throw light
on the present one. Lastly, it will systemati-

cally make use of and develop its capacity for accompanying and enforcing the dramatic gestures ; traces of which capacity have appeared often enough in the opera, but have there been left, like mimetics generally from which they arise, in an embryonic state, scarcely above the level of the pantomime. "On the one hand, as embodied harmony, it renders the distinct expression of melody possible, whilst on the other, it keeps the melody in the necessary uninterrupted flow, and thus always displays the motives of the dramatic action with the most convincing impressiveness to our feelings."

The entire work of art, then, intended by Wagner is *musical* in spirit, and could have been conceived by none but a man of universal artistic instincts, who is at the same time a great modern musician. Its mythical subject-matter, chosen because of its essentially emotional nature; its division into scenes, and the sequence of these ; the use of alliterative verse, and its melodious declamation ; the use of the orchestra, preparing, supporting, commenting, enforcing, recalling ; all its factors are imbued with the spirit of music. Their task is not accomplished if any one side of the subject remains to be supplied by some process of

abstract reasoning on the hearer's part. They
are to appeal exclusively to our feelings. The
sole test of what sort of thing is to be said
lies in the expressive power of music. Being
emotional throughout, the musical drama stands
higher as a form of art than the spoken play.
In it the profound pathos of dramatic speech
is not left to the discrimination of the individual
actor. The musician's sure *technique* positively
fixes every accent and every inflection, and a
composer in the act of conducting such a drama
is so completely in unison with the singers and
players, that one may talk without hyperbole
of an actual metempsychosis—his very soul
speaks from out of the performers.

Before concluding this division of the subject, let me express a hope that whoever has
read so far with some attention will be in a
position to see how inapplicable much of the
current talk about that great bugbear, "the
music of the future," is to Wagner and his
aims. His drama has nothing whatever to do
with the supposed reform—I say *supposed*
reform advisedly—of instrumental music which
has been dubbed "the music of the future."
Did any one ever dare to assert that the beautiful works of Schubert, Mendelssohn, Schu-

mann, &c., leave an unsatisfactory expression,
owing to any shortcomings capable of reform
in the manner of musical procedure employed
by these composers ? It is surely impossible
to see where reform is needed, and no musician
in his senses ever dreamt of attempting or
advocating such a thing; least of all Franz
Liszt, who is unhappily so often treated as the
wildest of the supposed destroyers of the beautiful—Liszt, who has on numberless occasions
proved his intimate knowledge of, and loyal
admiration for, the lovely works of Beethoven's
epigonæ. The innovations in details of form
and diction introduced by Berlioz and Liszt in
some of their instrumental works derive their
origin from Beethoven himself; they are the
result of a tendency which was carried out more
or less conscientiously by all his successors; it
is the desire of a *poetical basis* for instrumental
music. If such a desire be the distinctive
mark, surely Chopin, Schumann, Mendelssohn,
and all their living followers, are " musicians of
the future."

Be this as it may, Wagner's ideal drama is
a thing totally apart from this tendency towards
programme-music, the seeming contradictions of
which, from its high stand-point, it disposes of

with ease. Nor is Wagner's drama an attempt
at the reformation of the opera, though I have
spoken of it as the accomplished destiny of the
opera. It is no more a reformed opera than
man is a reformed monkey ; it can be measured
as little with an ordinary opera yard-stick as
with the conductor's-baton of an absolute musician. It is new from end to end, and it carries
its own criterion of excellence in the high and
intense emotions a correct performance of it
may and will arouse in every man who, in
Pistol's phrase, " hears with ears."

5

"Vates in propria patria honore caret."

"Tempo è galantuomo."

The theatre is the centre from which all truly national culture is diffused; no art can hope to lend effectual aid towards popular culture as long as the supreme importance of the theatre is unrecognised, as long as the theatre is not lifted from out of its present deplorable condition.

If the spirit of modern life, which takes its origin in the "renaissance," could succeed in producing a theatre that shall stand in relation to the innermost motives of modern culture as the Greek theatre stood to the religion of Greece, then the arts should have arrived at the same vivifying spring from which in Greece they nourished themselves; should this be impossible, "renascent" art has also had its day.

It is principally in the drama that the limitless capacities of music for emotional expression, the width and wealth of its resources are fully apparent; under the hands of great dramatic

*composers this capacity has grown in exact ratio
with the extent and the dignity of the opportu-
nities afforded to musicians by the dramatic poets;
and the future prospects of musical art are
intimately and indissolubly connected with those
of the theatre.*

These assertions can be taken as the *thesis*
which Wagner illustrates from numberless different points of view, in the many smaller writings which have the amelioration of the present
state of theatrical and musical things in Germany for an object. There are especially two
pamphlets :—" Bericht über eine in München
zu errichtende Deutsche Musikschule " (Report
concerning a German school of music to be
established at Munich), and " Ueber das Dirigiren " (On Conducting)—both small in bulk
but weighty in contents, from which I must
take a few gleanings, as in them the master's
dramatic ideal is brought to bear directly upon
questions of musical practice. If we remember
that it is from the high point of view of his
drama that he looks upon the musical doings
of the present, we shall be more inclined to
make allowances for the occasional hardness in
his criticism of contemporaneous efforts, and
for the extreme severity of his censure when

dealing with downright incapacity or wilful perversity.

Of the two pamphlets in question, the first is a scheme for the establishment of a school of music in Munich, the main object of which was to have been to train dramatic singers towards the correct presentation of works written in the German language, and in specifically German spirit ; and, together with this, to fix and to preserve a distinct and adequate style for the rendering of works by the great German composers, both vocal and instrumental. The second is a severe and elaborate criticism of the mode of conducting now current in Germany, with significant hints as to its improvement.

The school was not to teach all and everything, and end, as do most conservatoriums, by teaching little or nothing ; it was to devote itself exclusively to the attainment of *correct performances*—correct in every technical detail, and in every nuance of expression. The theory of harmony, counterpoint, and composition, history of music and æsthetics, even the exclusively technical side of the instructions for every particular instrument, were to be left to private tuition, under the supervision of the school authorities. It was intended to act direct upon the artistic taste and instinct of the pupils by means of constant united practice of the representative works of the great masters. There is, as every one knows, abundant opportunity in German towns to get excellent theoretical instruction; but what young musicians want above all things is a practical knowledge of the laws of beautiful and correct expression, and this the school was to cultivate.

That a knowledge of the laws of correct expression should be to some extent wanting to their performances is a truth which German musicians, and especially singers, do not like to hear, but the sense of which they are sometimes rather roughly taught by the public of Paris or London. There are many singers in Germany who deserve to be called good musicians; as a rule they know much more about music than their Italian or French brethren; they possess good voices too; yet they "cannot sing." The real cause of this, as of so many other practical shortcomings (and here is the point to which Wagner is ever returning), lies in the fact that Germany has never been in possession of a *national musical* theatre— a theatre which, acting

upon the national taste, and being in its turn
acted upon by the nation, should have developed
a *classical style of execution*, such as could ade-
quately reflect the pecular *German spirit* which
breathes in the great German poets and composers. The conservatoires of Naples, Milan,
and Paris preserved and fostered the styles
which had been developed by the artists of San
Carlo, of La Scala, and L'Académie de Musique,
with the co-operation of the Italian and French
nations. But the German theatres, unfortunately, having to cater for a public of Philistine
subscribers who attend all the year round, and
require constant change of diet, have never
subsisted on any speciality of their own ; they
produce every conceivable thing, from Sophocles
to the latest *cochonnerie à la* Offenbach. These
pieces are translated mostly by penny-a liners,
and are generally given without any attempt
at correctness of style. Whoever has passed
a year in Dresden, Berlin, or Vienna, can furnish a list of theatrical poltrooneries that makes
one's flesh creep. There are, of course, now
and then, exceptional performances, which are
prepared with due care, and are proportionately
good ; but these are inevitably swamped by the
numberless bad ones, and seem to have little

influence either upon the public or upon the artists immediately concerned.

It was objected that a German conservatorium need not trouble itself about Italian or French productions. " Let them go their ways —and let it conserve the proper tradition concerning Gluck and Mozart!"

Ay, but here lies the rub! The dramatic works of the Germans Gluck and Mozart must be studied with a view to French and Italian peculiarities of style; German singers have no more mastered these peculiarities than those of other works by entirely foreign authors. If Gluck and Mozart have ever been properly given in Germany, they certainly are not so now; and if proof were needed of the utter helplessness of the present race of operatic performers, one could not point to a more melancholy sight than their lifeless and colourless representations of *Don Giovanni* and *Iphigénie.*

It has also been objected that the real centre of musical life in Germany lies in the concert-room and not in the theatre. Granted; but it is impossible to deny that all the noble efforts which have been made by concert-givers and conductors, with a view to directing the taste of the nation towards the highest and the best, have been again and again disturbed by the overwhelming *miasma* arising from the theatrical morasses. You may witness after a Mozartian or Beethovenian symphony some *virtuoso* riding his parade horse, or some singer going through a series of contortions for the throat; whilst the public, demoralized by its daily meal of theatrical vulgarity and devoid of artistic instincts, applauds everything indiscriminately. The more one examines the matter, the more one's conviction grows that *if nobler and higher artistic tastes are to be effectively engrafted upon a nation,* there is but one way : *raise the quality and the character of theatrical performances.* And thus, to return to our starting point, the Munich institution was to prepare the material for a theatre in which the performances should be correct, and German.

Singing lessons are of the utmost importance to every young musician, no matter to what speciality he intends ultimately to devote himself, and the neglect of vocal studies is to be felt in Germany, not only with professed singers, but also with most instrumentalists and composers. Accordingly, elementary singing

instruction was to be made a *sine quâ non* for
every pupil of the school. In developing a
German style of singing, the peculiarities of the
language, its short and often mute vowels, its
clotted lumps of consonants, marvellously expressive though they be, its ever-recurring
gutturals and sibilants must be carefully taken
account of. For this reason, the prominent
feature of a German style, as opposed to the
long-drawn vocalism of the Italian style, must
of necessity consist in an energetic accentuation
akin to actual speech ; obviously a kind of
singing particularly well adapted to dramatic
delivery. When Wagner speaks of energetic
accents, he, of course, does not intend to sacri-
fice the beauty of sound pertaining to the
Italian method. The *cursus* was to combine
the study of Italian singing in the Italian language with German. Besides general instructions in music—harmony, counterpoint, and
composition, which, as has been already stated,
were to be left to private tuition—rhetoric and
gymnastics were to be added to the vocal
studies, so that in time the school for singing
might completely fulfil all the conditions necessary to the preparation of its pupils for the
lyric stage. The piano, that indispensable

auxiliary, and its literature, so important to musicians, were to receive due attention not only from those who wished to become *virtuosi*, but also from such as intended to devote themselves to composing and conducting. Finally, to give the tendencies of the school a chance of spreading more rapidly, a journal written by the masters, in which the novel tasks and problems emanating therefrom should be discussed, was to be published.

What has become of the school? It was started, and promised wonders. I was present at one of the examinations. It has not kept its promise since Wagner, and after him Von Bülow, left Munich.

The pamphlet on conducting should be translated entire. I shall pick out some points here and there, as it appears an impossible task to abridge or further condence it.

A true taste for classical compositions cannot accrue unless a truly classical style for their execution be developed. The general public accepts great works much more on authority than by reason of any emotional impressions the customary performances of them are capable of producing. Take a single example—Mozart's symphonies — notice two points : the vocal nature of the themes (in which respect he differs from and is superior to Haydn) and the sparse indications in the scores for the proper rendering of these. It is well known how hurriedly Mozart wrote his symphonies—generally for performance at some concert he was about to give—and how exacting he was as regards the rendering of his melodious phrases when rehearsing the orchestra. It is evident that the success of the performance depended in great measure upon the master's verbal admonitions ; and it is within the experience of every musician that even in our days, when the orchestral parts are overloaded with dynamical marks, a word from the conductor is more efficacious than written signs. Now, it is considered " classical " by nine conductors out of ten in Germany and elsewhere, to avoid most scrupulously all nuances of expression not expressly indicated in the score! And what becomes of Mozart's heavenly melodies under such a method of procedure ? He who was imbued with the noble spirit of older Italian singing, whose great merit it is to have transplanted its expressive inflections into the orchestra—what becomes of his themes if they are delivered without increase or decrease of accent, without

that modification of *tempo* and rhythm so indispensable to singers ?—what becomes of them
if they are played smoothly and neatly, like a
recitation of some rule-of-three sum ?

Beethoven's orchestral works are in a different, though not in a much better plight. His
scores contain ample directions for correct
execution ; still the difficulty of rendering his
symphonies properly is as much greater as his
thematic combinations are more elaborate than
Mozart's. New difficulties arise through the
peculiar use Beethoven makes of his rhythms ;
and to fix the proper *tempo* for his symphonic
movements, above all the ever-present delicate
and expressive *modification* of this tempo, without which the sense of many an eloquent phrase
remains incomprehensible, is a task requiring
artistic instincts such as the typical German
Kapellmeister is not as a rule remarkable for.

To my thinking the lively applause extremely lifeless orchestral performances of
Mozart's and Beethoven's symphonies are wont
to meet with would be utterly incomprehensible
if it were not for the fact that most people owe
their love for these works to numerous private
performances of pianoforte arrangements, so
that when they listen to the orchestra they are

already familiar with both themes and treatment, and the only access to their conception is
the vivid distinctness of orchestral colour.

The demand for continual though scarcely
perceptible modifications of tempo, such as inevitably ensue when music is executed in connection with a dramatic performance, forms the
essence of Wagner's pamphlet. He wishes to
see the *nuances* of tempo suggested by his dramatic instinct applied to pure instrumental
music, and it is very curious to note how the
results of this procedure chime with the descriptions that have come down to us of the
greatest musicians' manner of playing their
works, and of improvising—for instance, Schin-
dler's detailed account of Beethoven's rendering
of his sonatas and symphonies.

Conductors often miss the proper tempo
because they are ignorant of the art of singing,
for it is only after you have correctly caught
the *melos* (melodious phraseology) of a movement that you have found the *right tempo*.
The two are inseparable; one implies the other.
Older musicians rarely gave other than very
general indications : the two extremes, *allegro*,
adagio ; and *andante*, to denote the medium
between them. Sabastian Bach, in most cases,

gives no hints whatever, and this is, from a musical point of view, not without some show of reason. Bach may have said to himself :— He who does not understand my themes and their treatment, he whose instinct does not lead him to feel their character, what can he be expected to make of any vague Italian designation of tempo ?

The *tempo adagio* stands opposed to the *tempo allegro*, as the sustained tone to the animated movement (*figurirte Bewegung*). In the *tempo adagio*, as Beethoven has it, the sustained tone furnishes the laws for the movement. One might say, in a certain delicate sense, of the pure *adagio*, that it cannot be taken too slowly. Here the sustained tone speaks for itself; the smallest change of harmony is surprising, and successions the most remote are at once understood by our expectant feelings. Beethoven's *allegro* can be looked upon, also in a certain delicate sense, as the result of an admixture of the emotional *adagio* with *animated movement* (*bewegtere figuration*). In Beethoven's greatest *allegros* some large melody generally predominates, which in character is akin to the *adagio*, and which gives to these movements a certain *sentimental* colour (in the best acceptation of the word) that clearly distinguishes them from the earlier *naïve* sort of *allegro*. Take for example the opening melody of the Sinfonia Eroica or of the great trio in B flat. The exclusive character of the *naïve allegro* is not felt until much later in the course of these pieces, when the rhythmical movement gets the upper hand of the sustained tone. The best specimens of the *naïve allegro* are to be found in Mozart's *alla breve* movements, such as the *allegros* of the overtures—above all *Figaro* and *Don Giovanni*. In pieces of this character, of which Beethoven too furnishes specimens, like the *finale* of his symphony in A major, the rhythmical movement has it all its own way— celebrates its orgies as it were ; and it is impossible to take these pieces too quick, or with too much decision. But whatever lies between the two extremes stands under the laws of *mutual relationship, each to the other*, and requires as many and as delicate combinations of tempo as are the nuances and inflections of which the sustained tone is capable.

We find in *Beethoven's* sentimental *allegro* all the separate peculiarities of the older *allegro*, the sustained and the broken tone, the vocal *portamento* and the animated movement, so fused as to make an inseparable, sole, and unique musical tissue ; and it is undeniably certain that all the manifold materials which go to make up one of his symphonic movements must be rendered in accordance with their respective nature, if the whole is not to make an impression somewhat akin to that of a monstrosity. Wagner recounts how in his youth he had often seen older musicians shake their heads over the Eroica. Dionys Weber, for example, who was director of the conservatorium at Prague, treated it altogether as a nonentity. He knew of nothing beyond the Mozartian *naïve allegro* spoken of above ; and whoever heard the pupils of his school play the first movement of the Eroica in the strict *tempo* proper to that Mozartian *allegro* was certainly constrained to agree with him. Have we, since, improved much upon Dionys' mode of procedure ?

In connection with his assertion, that as regards tempo everything depends upon the executants understanding the melodious phraseology of a piece, Wagner goes on to show how great a risk conductors run who, of a sudden, expect their orchestra to play a piece in a different tempo from the supposed " traditional ', one. The deplorable fact is, he says, that a mode of playing, which can be described as "a careless gliding over things," has taken root which is intimately connected with the incorrect tempo habitually taken for certain movements— witness the third movement of Beethoven's 8th Symphony, which, though expressly marked *Tempo di Menuetto*, is almost invariably served up as a sort of *scherzo*.

Nothing is less familiar to German orchestras than the production of *a long-sustained tone with unflagging strength*. Ask any orchestral instrument for a full, equal, and sustained *forte*, and the player will be astonished at the unusual demand! *Yet this equally-sustained tone is the basis of all dynamics*—as with singing so with orchestral playing. Without this basis an orchestra will produce much noise but no *power*. But our conductors think very highly of an *over-delicate piano*, which the strings produce without the slightest trouble, but which for the wind, and especially the wood wind instruments, is extremely difficult to attain. The players on these latter, particularly flutists, who have transformed their instruments, formerly so soft, into " forcible tubes," find it scarcely possible to produce a delicately-sustained *piano*— with perhaps the exception of French oboists, who have never altered the pastoral character of their instrument, or of clarinettists, if you ask them for the " echo effect."

Now the discrepancies between the *piano* of the winds and that of the strings seem entirely to escape the observation of conductors. It is the character of the *piano* of the strings which is in a great measure at the bottom of the fault, for we are as much without a *proper piano* as we are without a *proper forte; both lack fulness of tone.* The fiddlers, who find it so easy to draw their bows over the strings so as to produce a whispering vibration, might copy the full-toned *piano* from exceptionally good wind instrument players. These again might gain by imitating the *piano* of great singers. For these two, the full *piano* and sustained *forte*, are, to reitterate our dogma, the two poles of orchestral dynamics between which all execution should move. United to the proper *tempo* they form the elements of a truly classical style for the delivery of instrumental music.

In the face of all these troubles, one cannot shrink from the confession that there is very serious danger in advocating *modification of tempo.* Are we to allow, it may be asked,

every man who "wags a stick" to do as it
listeth him with the *tempi* of our glorious instrumental music? Are we to permit him to
"make effects" in Beethoven's symphonies as
his reckless fancy may dictate? To which I
know of no answer, except it be, 'Tis a pity
men should occupy positions they are not fit
for.

"Ueber das Dirigiren" contains numerous
examples in musical type; amongst others,
many details concerning the interpretation of
the overtures to *Der Freischütz* and *Die Meistersinger*, Beethoven's 3rd, 5th, 8th, and 9th Symphonies, &c.

Concerning this pamphlet, and in fact concerning *all* Wagner's writings, I would say
what the supernatural voice is reported to have
said to the Father of the Church, St. Augus-
tine : *Tolle, lege*—take and read.

6.

—

"Natura lo fece e poi ruppe lo stampo."
Ariosto.

IT is humiliating to confess, after all is said
and done, that neither an exposition of artistic
theories nor any species of critical and æsthetical talk can finally settle a single vital point
in art matters—the actual works of art must in
the end be left to speak for themselves.

In the life of a man of abnormal receptive
powers, the centre of gravity of whose existence must be looked for in the realms of thought
rather than in the realms of action, biographical
facts are far less significant and worthy of attention than they would be in the life of a man
of the world, whose practical doings represent
the sum total of his existence. The strivings
more or less successful of a man of genius for
the acquisition of the necessary *quantum* of
daily bread and butter are of less than second-
ary importance. Nevertheless, as it always
pleasant, and sometimes even useful, to know
where, when, or how he bore the burden of
professional work, though such knowledge can-

not in any sense widen one's conception of the man's nature or of his exceptional powers, I propose to furnish, by way of *opus supereroga-tionis*, a number of biographical facts which may serve as landmarks to the outward history of Wagner's artistic career.

He has become a European celebrity in spite of himself. I say in spite of himself advisedly, for to those who believe in him and his works there is nothing more humiliating than the fact that the interest excited by his name is not one which derives from his works, but rather from his personality. Outside of Germany his reputation rests, if the truth must be told, on his mistakes of policy. "*Il a les défauts de ses vertus*," as Madame de Staël, and and George Sand after her, has it. Like most men of genius when they meddle in practical matters, he is apt to make a mountain of a molehill ; and the scandal arising from a number of momentary exaggerations on his part, fostered as it has been by the attack of a hostile press, is in reality the cause of his name being in everybody's mouth. His dramas, and especially the later ones, are unfortunately as yet in no danger of being too familiar out of Germany.

Apropos of the position of a man of genius in this world of mental distress and physical want, let me be allowed to translate some lines from the second volume of Arthur Schopenhauer's " Die Welt als Wille und Vorstellung :" " All great theoretical feats of whatever sort are achieved by means of so powerful, firm, and exclusive a concentration of their author's mind towards one particular object, that for the time being all the rest of the world disappears completely, and the one object becomes the sole reality to him. This great and forcible concentration, which is one of the special privileges of genius, is by no means rare even in the presence of ordinary things, and in the affairs of daily life ; and under such a focus these latter are often enormously exaggerated, much as a flea takes elephantine proportions under the microscope. It is for this reason that highly-gifted persons are violently affected, rendered sad, gay, thoughtful, timid, angry, &c., by things which would not touch an ordinary mortal. For this reason also genius is wanting in *sobriety*, in the power of seeing in things, at least as far as our personal aims are concerned, nothing beyond what is contained in them. How much common sense, quiet composure, entire sereneness and evenness of conduct a man of ordinary capacity exhibits in comparison with a man of genius! Yet it is the latter, so frequently sunk in dreams, or excited by passion, from whose restless anguish and pain immortal works spring forth. Genius stands almost invariably in an equivocal relation to the surrounding world, for its very strivings and doings are, as a rule, in opposition to and at war with the age. Men of mere talent always turn up at the proper time; they are moved by the spirit of their age and called forth by its requirements; they are able to satisfy these and no more; they take their share in the course of contemporaneous development, or by their help some special science advances a step or two; and they reap rewards and gain due applause. But to the next generation their works are no longer palateable, and must be replaced by others, which again in their turn do not last. Genius, on the contrary, flashes upon the times like a comet upon the planets' orbits, to the well-regulated and visible order of which its completely eccentric course is quite alien; it cannot therefore chime in with the course of regular development of the age, but it throws its works out far ahead (as the *im-*

perator who devotes himself to death throws his spear among the enemy) where time alone can overtake them. Its relations to the men of talent, whose career culminates in the meanwhile, is well expressed in the words of the evangelist—' My time is not yet come, but your time is always ready.' (St. John vii. 6.)"

But to begin with our biographical facts. I have gathered them here and there, mainly however, from a little autobiographical sketch which appeared many years ago in the *Zeitung für die elegante Welt*, the editor of which, Laub, was a friend of Wagner's, and induced him to furnish a number of data, with a view to their being arranged for his journal. But Wagner's sketch struck him as being so bright and fresh that he chose to print it intact.

Wilhelm Richard Wagner was born 22nd May, 1813, at Leipzig. His father, an *actuarius* of police, died six months after, and the widow was re-married to Ludwig Geyer, an actor, painter, and author of comedies, who also died early—when Richard was seven years of age. It had been his intention to bring up Richard as a painter, but the boy proved invincibly awkward at drawing; so he did at pianoforte playing, in which, some months before Geyer's decease, he had a few lessons. The teacher caught him hammering at tunes from the overture to *Der Freischütz* with monstrous fingering in lieu of practising his exercises, and pronounced him a hopeless case; which dictum has since proved right enough, for Wagner continues to this day to torture the piano in a most abominable fashion.

The fact that he was *not* an "infant phenomenon" is nowise surprising if the strangely original nature of his gifts be considered. To my mind, sneers at the astonishing number of musical prodigies are perfectly legitimate; let it only be borne in mind that he who sneers is wrong if he represents the faculties required for music as being of a lower order than those required for other arts. To account for the presence of so many prodigies it is sufficient to point out, besides the hunger of indigent parents and the vanity of wealthier ones, that no art has in the course of time become so petrified in its rules and forms of procedure as music; and, moreover, that people are ready to hail any youth found capable of handling a few of these forms with some ease as a composer, whilst they would not dream of calling this or that boy a poet merely because he was able to make stanzas with the correct numbers of syllables in each line. It is neither easier nor more difficult to master all the means of expression in music than in any other art, only as regards music a very large proportion of the public are still in a state of childhood; they revel in sounds, leaving the sense to take care of itself.

Music, then, though he was enthusiastic about it, was but an accessory to Wagner's studies; Greek, Latin, mythology, and ancient history being the main points at the Kreuz Schule of Dresden, which he attended with a view to the usual university career. He was given to poetising, sketched tragedies in Greek form, and passed muster in the school for a clever fellow *in literis*. He learnt English so as to be able to read Shakespeare properly, and he translated bits in metre. He projected an immense tragedy, which he describes as a concoction made up of *Hamlet* and *King Lear*, on an absurdly grand scale. Forty-two men died in the course of it, and he was obliged to make a number of them return as ghosts, so as to keep the last acts sufficiently stocked with *dramatis personæ*. During two years this production occupied him; he left Dresden while

it was still progressing and returned to Leipzig,
where, at the *Gewandhaus* concerts, he first
received intense impressions from the instrumental works of Beethoven and Mozart; and,
in imitation of the former's *Egmont*, he attempted to add music to his play. When this
play was at length discovered by his family
to have led him to neglect his philological
studies, there was, as usual in such cases, a grand
quarrel, followed by endless minor recrimina-
tions. But he was not to be stopped; he
wrote overtures for grand orchestra, a sonata, a
quartett, &c. One overture, which he describes
as the culminating point of his musical absurdi-
ties, was performed and ridiculed at the Leipzig
Theatre. Whilst he was a student at the
University of Leipzig he went through a strict
course of contrapunctal studies with Theodor
Weinlig, then cantor at the Thomas-schule,
and an excellent musician, which laid a solid
foundation for his musical future. Under the
supervision of Weinlig, he brought forth a
considerable number of works, amongst which
a symphony, an overture, and the libretto together with some musical numbers for a tragic
opera, are mentioned. The overture was performed at the *Gewandhaus* with encouraging

success—and the symphony pleased at Prague and Leipzig. Mozart and Beethoven, especially the latter—for whose works he had at that time already the most passionate admiration—were his models. "I doubt," writes Heinrich Dorn, in an article published in Schumann's *Neue Zeitschrift für Musik* (1838, No. 7), whether there ever was a young musician who knew Beethoven's works more thoroughly than Wagner at his eighteenth year. The master's overtures and larger instrumental compositions he had copied for himself in score. He went to sleep with the sonatas and rose with the quartetts—he sang the songs and whistled the concertos (for his pianoforte playing was never of the best)—in short, he was possessed with a *furor teutonicus*, which, added to a high education and a rare mental activity, promised to bring forth rich fruit." In 1833 he was at Würzburg, composing an opera in three acts, *Die Feen*, for which he had contrived a libretto after Gozzi's *Woman-Snake*, and conducting the chorus at the theatre. His next opera, *Das Liebesverbot*, after Shakespeare's *Measure for Measure*, was written while he was conductor at Magdeburg, and performed in 1836, after only twelve days' preparation, with *nil* for a result, as might have been expected. Soon after this the Magdeburg Theatre failed, and Wagner, penniless and encumbered with debts, after a visit to Berlin, whither a fruitless hope of having his opera performed had led him, accepted the conductorship at a theatre at Königsberg. There, in 1836, he married, and composed two overtures, " Polonia " and " Rule, Britannia." In 1837, whilst conducting the theatre at Riga, he began sketching the five-act tragic opera, *Rienzi*, the first of his dramatic works which has gained acceptance in Germany and has been published. Its libretto, based on Bulwer's novel, is laid out on an immense scale so as to make it suitable for the very largest theatres only. With the music to two acts of it finished he started in 1839, without funds or friends, and without the smallest definite plan of action, for Paris. At Boulogne he made Meyerbeer's acquaintance, who, on seeing the score of *Rienzi*, furnished him with letters of introduction to the musical and theatrical notabilities of Paris. In consequence of these, things looked bright for a little time, but he soon found that to gain a hearing in Paris without the aid of influential friends on the spot (Meyerbeer did not stay there for any length of time during the two years of Wagner's sojourn) was an Herculean task, beyond the reach even of such indomitable energy as his. When things looked particularly black he took to writing articles for Schlesinger's *Gazette Musicale*, and making arrangements of operas—Halévy's *Reine de Chypre*, Donizetti's *Favorita*, and the like for the pianoforte and all other instruments, the cornet-à-piston among the number. Some of the articles into which he threw a good deal of his personal experience, such as "Das Ende eines deutschen Musikers in Paris," or of his *then* paradoxical opinions and fantastic aspirations, as in "Eine Pilgerfahrt zu Beethoven," created a considerable sensation. About this time the text-book to *Der fliegende Holländer* was conceived, and the music to it executed in the short space of seven weeks. There is a story current about this opera, to the effect that it was written to the order of Monsieur Léon Pillet, director of the Grand Opéra, and was rejected on account of the miserable quality of the music, which may as well be set to rights. The fact is that Wagner for a long time was led to expect that he might receive an order to compose an opera, and he had, in this expectation, handed to Monseiur Pillet a sketch of *Der fliegende Holländer.* But Pillet procrastinated from month to month, until Wagner happened to be informed by a friend that his sketch had been been put into the hands of a professional librettist. He then, not to be entirely swindled, thought it best to sell his versified rendering of the sketch outright, and to let a musician appointed by Pillet (called Dietsch) maltreat it at his discretion. In the meanwhile he pleased himself by setting it to music for his own private edification. Giving up all hopes of Paris, he sent the score of *Rienzi* to the Court Theatre at Dresden. It was accepted, performed with immense success in 1842, and Wagner, who had followed it to Dresden, found himself of a sudden the most popular man there, and the King of Saxony's Hofcapellmeister. On the 2nd of January, 1843, *Der fliegende Holländer* was produced at Dresden.

That part of Wagner's career which is of universal interest commences with *Der fliegende Holländer,* and it would be a delightful task, if one had sufficient leisure, to trace, through *Tannhäuser, Lohengrin, Die Meistersinger, Tristan und Isolde,* and *Der Ring des Nibelungen,* the gradual expanse of his artistic practice. Here a few dates must suffice. While engaged

among the arduous duties of a principal conductorship at Dresden, *Tannhäuser* was completed and performed in 1845. *Das Liebesmahl
der Apostel,* a large Biblical *scena* for male voices
and orchestra, and *Lohengrin,* were finished in
1847 ; and before the revolution in 1849 the
poem of *Die Meistersinger* (which was originally
intended to form a sort of comical pendant to
Tannhäuser) and of *Siegfrieds Tod* were written.
The revolution, in which Wagner took active
part with written and spoken addresses, put an
end to the connection with Dresden ; he fled,
and found refuge in Zürich. During the next
ten years he appeared before the public, if we
except a few concerts which he conducted here
and there—for instance, the eight concerts of
the London Philharmonic Society, in the season
of 1855—only as a writer on musical æsthetics.
" Die Kunst und die Revolution," "Das Kunstwerk der Zukunft," and " Oper und Drama "
appeared in 1849, 1850, and 1851 respectively.
During his sojourn at Zürich also the poem of
Der Ring des Nibelungen, consisting of *Das
Rheingold, Die Walküre, Siegfried, Götterdämmerung*—which, of all his works, is the most
colossal in dimensions—was finished. He has
since completed the scores of the three first

parts of this tetralogy, and is now at work on the final act of the fourth. In 1857, also, the poem of *Tristan* was begun, and the music to it finished two years later, during his prolonged stay at Venice. Towards the end of 1859 he came to Paris, and in February, 1860, gave three concerts there. On the 13th of March, 1861, *Tannhäuser* was produced at the Grand Opéra, with a masterly translation by Edmond Roche, at the command of the emperor, and hooted and whistled off the stage by the members of the Jockey Club. In 1863, he appeared at Vienna, Prague, Leipzig, St. Petersburg, Moscow, Pesth, &c., conducting orchestral concerts with brilliant success ; and in May, 1864, King Ludwig II. called him to Munich, where in 1865 *Tristan*, in 1868 *Die Meistersinger*, in 1869 *Das Rheingold*, in 1870 *Die Walküre* (the latter two without the composer's co-operation), were first performed. In August, 1870, he was married a second time, to Cosima von Bülow, *née* Liszt.

His artistic career is about to reach its culminating point in 1874, when his most gigantic achievement, the Trilogy, "der Ring des Nibelungen," consisting of " Die Walküre," " Siegfried," " Götterdämmerung," with a preparatory evening, "das Rheingold," is to be produced under his personal supervision at a theatre specially designed for the purpose and now in course of erection at Bayreuth. The funds for this purpose, some 300,000 Thalers, are being furnished by different "Wagner Societies" which have sprung up spontaneously, absolutely without agitation on the master's part, and in most instances without his knowledge, in all parts of Germany, in London, Pesth, Milan, New York, &c. It is the object of these Societies to give him a chance of performing his work correctly, and in every respect as he has conceived it; for which, as long as the present state of things at all German court and town theatres continues, there would have been little or no chance.

COMPLETE LIST OF
RICHARD WAGNER'S PUBLICATIONS,
I.—MUSICAL WORKS.

(*a*) FOR THE STAGE :

Rienzi, der letzte der Tribunen. First performed under Wagner, 1842, Dresden.

Der fliegende Holländer. First performed under Wagner, 1843, Dresden.

Tannhäuser. First performed under Wagner, 1845, Dresden
(The French Edition, translated by Edmond Roche, Paris 1861, contains the opening scenes, Act I., as they were re-written and enlarged for the Grand Opéra.)

Lohengrin. First performed under Liszt, 1850, Weimar.

Tristan und Isolde. First performed under von Bülow 1865, Munich.

Die Meistersinger von Nürnberg. First performed under Bülow, 1868, Munich.

Der Ring des Nibelungen. Ein Bühnenfestspiel.

   1. Das Rheingold. Attempted 1869, Munich.
   2. Die Walküre. Attempted 1870, Munich.
   3. Siegfried.
   4. Götterdämmerung (nearly finished).

(The whole to be performed at Bayreuth, 1874.)

(*b*) FOR CHORUS AND ORCHESTRA :

An Webers Grabe. Dresden, 1844 (on occasion of the burial of Weber's remains, which had been brought from London.)

Das Liebesmahl der Apostel. Eine Biblische Scene. Dresden, 1847. Male chorus and orchestra.

(*c*) ORCHESTRAL PIECES :

Eine Faustouverture. 1839.
Huldigungsmarsch. 1869.
Kaisermarsch. 1871.
Close to Gluck's overture *Iphigénie en Aulide*.

(*d*) SONGS :

Les deux Grenadiers. Paris, 1839
Dors mon Enfant. Paris, 1839) Republished, with
Mignonne. Paris, 1839   } German translation,
Attente. Paris, 1839   ) Berlin, Fürstner, 1871.
Fünf Gedichte. 1860.

   1. Der Engel. 2. Stehe still. 3. Im Treibhaus.
   4. Schmerzen. 5. Träume. (London and Mayence: Schott & Co.)

(*e*) PIANOFORTE PIECES :

Sonata, B flat. 1832.
Polonaise in 4 mains. 1832.
Albumblatt. 1861.

B.—*LITERARY WORKS.*

(Collected Edition in nine volumes, now in course of publication. Leipzig : Fritzsch.)

1. Autobiographische Skizze (bis 1842).

Das Liebesverbot. Bericht über eine erste opernauffürung.

Rienzi, der letzte der Tribunen.

Ein deutscher Musiker in Paris. Novellen und Aufsätze.

    1. Eine Pilgerfahrt zu Beethoven.

    2. Ein Ende in Paris.

    3. Ein glücklicher Abend.

    4. Ueber deutsches Musikwesen.

    5. Der Virtuos und der Künstler.

    6. Der Künstler und die öffentlichkeit.

    7. Rossini's *Stabat Mater.*

Ueber die Ouvertüre.

Der Freischütz in Paris.

    1. Der Freischütz. An das Pariser Publicum.

    2. *Le Freyschutz.* Bericht nach Deutschland.

Bericht über eine neue Pariser Oper. (*La reine de Chypre*). Von Halévy.

} 1839-41,

Der fliegende Holländer.

2. Tannhäuser und der Sängerkrieg auf der Wartburg.

Bericht über die Heimbringung der sterblichen Ueberreste Karl Maria von Weber's aus London nach Dresden. 1844.

    Rede an Weber's letzten Ruhestätte.

    Gesang nach der Bestattung.

Bericht über die Aufführung der neunten Symphonie von Beethoven im Jahre 1846, nebst Programm dazu.

Lohengrin.

Die Wibelungen. Weltgeschichte aus der Sage. 1848.

Der Nibelungenmythus. Als Entwurf zu einem Drama.

Siegfrieds Tod. [1848.

Trinkspruch am Gedenktage des 300 jährigen Bestehens der Königlich sächsischen Kapelle in Dresden.

Entwurf zur Organisation eines deutschen Nationaltheatres für das Königreich Sachsen. 1849.

3. Die Kunst und die Revolution. 1849.

Das Kunstwerk der Zukunft. 1850.

" Wieland der Schmiedt," als Drama entwurfen.

Kunst und Klima. 1850.

4. Oper und Drama. 1851.

    Erster Theil : Die Oper und das Wesen der Musik.

    Zweiter Theil : Des Schauspiel und das Wesen der Dramatischen Dicht-Kunst.

    Dritter Theil : Dichtkunst und Tonkunst im Drama der-Zukunft.

Eine Mittheilung an meine Freunde. 1851.

5. Ueber die "Goethestiftung." Brief an Franz Liszt. 1851.

Ein Theatre in Zürich. 1851.

Ueber Musikalische Kritik. Brief an den Herausgeber der " Neuen Zeitschrift für Musik." 1852.

Das Judenthum in der Musik. 1852.

Errinnerungen an Spontini.

Nachruf an L. Spohr und Chordirector W. Fischer. 1860.

Gluck's Ouvertüre zu " Iphigenie in Aulis." 1854.

Ueber die Aufführung des " Tannhäuser."

Bemerkungen zur Aufführung der Oper : Der Fliegende Holländer.

Programmatische Erläuterungen :

    1. Beethoven's " Heroische Symphonie."

    2. Ouvertüre zu " Koriolan."

    3. Ouvertüre zum " Fliegenden Holländer."

    4. Ouvertüre zum " Tannhäuser."

    5. Vorspiel zu " Lohengrin."

Ueber Franz Liszt's Symphonische Dichtungen.

6. Der Ring des Nibelungen, ein Bühnenfestpiel.
   Vorabend : Das Rheingold.
   Erster Tag : Die Walküre.
   Zweiter Tag : Siegfried.
   Dritter Tag : Götterdämmerung.
   Epilogisher Bericht über die Umstände und Schicksale,
      welche die Aufführung des Bühnenfestspieles "Der
      Ring des Nibelungen, bis zur Veröffentlichung der
      Dichtung desselben begleiteten.
7. Eine wichtige Frage der Musik der Gegenwart.
   Brief über Liszt's Instrumentalcompositionen.
   Tristan und Isolde.
   Brief an Berlioz. 1860.
   Zukunftsmusik. 1864.
   Bericht über die Aufführung des " Tannhäuser " in Paris.
8. Die Meistersinger von Nürnberg.   [1861.
   Das Wiener Hofopernthcater. 1863.
   Gedicht an Ludwig II., König von Bayern.
   Ueber Staat und Religion.
   Einladung zur Aufführung des Tristan in München.
   Erinnerungen an Ludwig Schnorr von Carolsfeld.
   Bericht über eine in München zu errichtende Musikschule.
   Was ist Deutsch ?   [1865.
9. Deutsche Kunst und deutsche Politik. 1868.
   Vermischte Aufsätze.
      1. H. Riehl.
      2. Ferdinand Hiller.
      3. Erinnerungen an Rossini.
      4. Studie über den Schreibestyl der " Jetztzeit."
      5. Brief an Frau M. v. M.
      6. Errinnerungen an Auber.
   Ueber das Dirigiren. 1870.
   Beethoven. 1870.
   Ueber die Bestimmung der Oper. 1871.
   Ueber Schauspieler und Sänger. 1872.